The Hat of My Mother

The Hat of My Mother

Stories by
Max Steele

Algonquin Books of Chapel Hill   1994

Published by
Algonquin Books of Chapel Hill
Post Office Box 2225
Chapel Hill, North Carolina 27515-2225
a division of
Workman Publishing Company, Inc.
708 Broadway
New York, New York 10003

First Front Porch Paperback Edition, April 1994. Originally published in
hardcover by Algonquin Books of Chapel Hill in 1988.

Some of the stories in this book, many in different form, first appeared in
other publications: "The Hat of My Mother" (under the title "My Moth-
er's Night Out") and "The Girl from Carthage," *McCall's*; "The Glass-
Brick Apartment" and "Forget the Geraniums," *Harper's*; "Another Love
Story," *Redbook*; "What to Do Till the Postman Comes," *Paris Review*;
"Where She Brushed Her Hair" (under the title "Fiction, Fact and
Dream") and "The Man in the Doll House," *Carolina Quarterly*; "The
Cat and the Coffee Drinkers," *The New Yorker*; "Ah Love! Ah Me!," *Col-
lier's*; "The Silent Scream," *Esquire*; "Color the Daydream Yellow," *Quar-
terly Review of Literature*; and "The Tin Can," *Delta Epsilon Sigma Journal.*

Library of Congress Cataloging-in-Publication Data
Steele, Max, 1922–
    The hat of my mother.
    I. Title.
PS3537.T27825H38   1988   813'.54   87-28995
ISBN 1-56512-076-0

10 9 8 7 6 5 4 3 2 1

For Kevin Russell Steele

Contents

The Hat of My Mother

MY MOTHER, if she were alive today, would be ninety years old, my father a hundred. In the forty years they were married, my mother spent only one night away from home without him and that was the day she was kidnapped.

To understand how a woman like her could be taken away, you would need to understand how deeply she believed in manners. Manners and courage, she felt, would take one safely through any situation. Once, for instance, during the Depression, a terrible-looking white man, tattooed and scarred, appeared at our back door and demanded food, good food, not any corn bread scraps and hominy, he wanted a full meal. My mother stood close to the screen door, locking it while holding his eyes steadily with hers and saying: "Why certainly, but you must come around to the dining room off the side porch, we never serve anyone in the kitchen."

She stood in the bay window of the dining room and watched him pull on the door which had not been opened all summer. The porch roof had been leaking, and the tongue-and-groove porch floor had swollen and buckled.

I

"Now," she said, firmly through the window, "I don't believe I know you, do I? I don't remember ever seeing your face or hearing your name before."

He allowed, in a Northern industrial accent, as how he didn't give a damn for the South and such formalities, that it was food and plenty of it he was after.

"Perhaps you have the wrong house," she said. "Maybe I should call the police. I'm sure they'd be glad to help you find your friends."

The sanity in her voice and the calmness in her eyes brought sanity to his face. He stepped back, blinked at the door, surveyed the porch, said he believed she was right, he didn't remember any side porch, but not to bother, the house he was looking for must be on the next block over. He stepped back down the steps and she walked quickly and locked the front door while watching him running across the lawn and down the gravel drive and through the grillwork gate beyond the boxwoods.

She had often hired worse-looking men to cut the grass, dig up the garden, or do any sort of outside work, and had never had any trouble with anyone except my father, who was not so sure that good manners were all the protection one needed in a Southern town which had grown so large he could no longer identify everyone in it by sight or hearsay. With the cigarette factory laying off, there were some mean-looking drifters arriving every day and angry they'd come so far to work when there was no work.

My mother, though, was supremely confident in her own home. Outside of it she became a different person: an actress who hid her natural shyness by a graceful, but not haughty, upward tilt of her chin and a way of walking usually reserved for aisles. Ladies, after a certain age, she felt should be seen at church, if they liked going to church, which she didn't, weddings if the bride was the daughter of a close relative or friend, and funerals of those few people one had known twenty years or longer. Funerals and weddings of prominent people were to be avoided, "If you wouldn't be among the first twenty-five asked, you don't belong there." In such cases she "sent": flowers, food, and any handmade object. But the present should represent a sacrifice of time, or money, or thought. New clothes were to be worn several times at home before being worn in public. In that way they did not seem "new" and one could be quite at ease and natural in them. In general she disliked anything that was for the purpose of impressing others or calling attention to oneself.

Her one exception was an indulgence in hats. Because of the special angle and tilt of her head and her rather handsome profile, she wore hats well. She bought few of them but they were expensive and they lasted ten and twenty and sometimes thirty years. Somewhere I have read that women always retain in their style some aspect of dress which was in fashion during the time of their first or greatest love. My mother and father were married in 1910 and she retained always, especially in her summer hats, something of the Gibson Girl aspect. Soon after the First World War she had bought an extremely becoming one, broad-brimmed and almost all flowers which, except for once or twice a year, stood with her two other hats in her hat closet.

In 1933 the hat was so old and so much a trademark that it was a joke in the family. The year before she had promised my father to replace it, and on one spring visit to town she had tried to buy a new one and had not found another one well-made enough to have trimmed. When she returned that day to put on her ancient hat she could not find it, and Mr. Ramsey and all the salespeople were embarrassing her by the fuss they were making in their search for it. She had slipped out of the store and there in the window was her twelve-year-old hat where the new window dresser was featuring it in a display.

The following year, the year she was kidnapped, she promised my father again that she would replace it. Mr. Ramsey had told her there was a lady in town who would know how to trim one properly if she could find one the shape she liked.

My mother shopped twice a year at the oldest stores.

Once in August for school clothes for the younger children, and once at Mardi Gras to buy materials for the older girls' Easter clothes. Her shopping, even on those two occasions when she would venture downtown, was done largely over the telephone. For a week or so before each outing, she would telephone the few stores which she felt still carried items of quality and would ask to speak to the owner of the store or to one of the oldest salespeople. She would say: "Mrs. Henley, I am going to be coming in on Tuesday, and I wonder if you could have some wool challis to show me in a houndstooth or in a solid Cambridge grey." Or: "Mr. Hodges, this is Mrs. B. F. Russell. Last fall when I was in, you said you had ordered some French kid gloves such as you used to carry." Many of the things she ordered were imported and hard to find, but in the long run, because they lasted forever, not as expensive as "stylish, thrown-together-for-the-moment" clothes. We did not have many clothes and we hated them from the beginning because they would last and be handed down and down and down.

But that Tuesday morning in late March, her telephone shopping done, my mother opened the door for Mrs. Honeycutt, which we all thought was a fine name for a dressmaker. Mrs. Honeycutt whistled, very unladylike, through the gap in her front teeth, as she brought in her sewing machines, scissors, baskets and cushions and special chair. She set up shop in the alcove upstairs. We were allowed to go into the sewing attic and roll the dressmaker dummies down the long hall to her and to help her set up the ironing boards and sewing tables. My mother brought out button boxes and old dresses from which the laces and furs and buttons were to be removed. She would be leaving Mrs. Honeycutt with enough work to keep her busy this first day of a sewing week.

Before the Depression my father had always sent a car to take my mother to town; later she had called cabs; but today she was going by streetcar. Regardless of how she travelled to town, she always walked the two miles home. She shopped only at stores that still delivered and therefore never carried any packages.

It was always a moment of adventure when she finally walked across the porch, still giving instructions to the cook and to each of the children about what was to be accomplished and what left undone during her absence. This morning she was especially cheerful and promised to return with a new hat. She was very much against spending the money she had saved (in a basket in the hat closet) for a hat when we needed so many other things. But after all, she had been putting odd change there for more than six years and if that was what everyone wanted most she would do it. She wore a black cloche and carried the old flowered hat with her to find another as much like it as possible. She planned as usual to walk home.

Late that afternoon my father was sitting on the porch, pretending to read the paper, but looking up constantly to see if he could see her rounding the corner and coming into sight. There was a thunderstorm in the air and he was a little worried. The rain began and he ran immediately to the drive and drove off looking for her.

He came back after going only to the streetcar stop. "She'll have sense enough to get inside," he said. The storm lasted until dark and she was still not home. My father began walking through the house from room to room. And then he began telephoning every store he knew she might have been in. Some of them were closed already and he called the owners at their homes. Finally he learned that she had left Hodges and Swensons to find a French woman who lived in the old Mayberry Smith house and trimmed hats. My father could not find the number and so rushed off again to fetch my mother.

He came home alone. Between then and the time we were sent to bed at nine he was in and out of the house, phoning, demanding that various proprietors reopen their stores to see if by chance she had been locked in a dressing room. He found the man who had sold her a hat and had sent her on her way to the French milliner. Before three-thirty that afternoon. Only two blocks from the store. Within those two blocks she had disappeared. My father, at one moment furious and the next dead-white, called the police. He then sent us off to our rooms. We were to be asleep when she got home. Just as if nothing had happened. That, he was saying in a miserable voice, was what she would want.

THE NEXT morning we were waked, as usual, at seven. My father was already up and dressed and walking about the house, grinning, talking, laughing. The dining room smelled of hot biscuits and ham. The cook was singing in the kitchen, and Mrs. Honeycutt was having breakfast on a tray in the sewing alcove. My mother, in the clothes she had worn to town the day before, was sitting at her desk, counting little piles of change, and sorting bills, and sipping her early morning tea.

One by one, as we came down, we asked if she had really been kidnapped, if my father had found her, when had she gotten home, how had she gotten home, had the police found her, and did she have a new hat? To all these questions my mother said: "I will tell you when we're all ready to sit down."

Seated, she at one end of the table, my father at the bay window end, two children on one side, three on the other, she said she would tell it once, and then she did not want to hear any more about it ever from any of us, and certainly she had better not ever hear of it from anyone outside the family. She looked each of us directly in the eye and we each nodded. It was understood: no one would speak of it again. She began by waiting for my father to quit smiling and then she began in a quick, reasonable voice, to recite her story:

I shopped awhile at Hodges and Swensons where the streetcar let me out and saw Mrs. Jones at Pride and Patton and then went on down to have the setting secured on my ring at Hellam's, and told them I'd be back after lunch to pick it up. And then I crossed over and did some shopping on the sunny side and spoke to Mrs. Latham and had lunch at a tea room in the Farmer's Bank Building, the small room where I used to do my banking, but apparently now men and women are all going to bank together.

After lunch I walked a bit, just noticing all the changes, how many of the beautiful old homes have been torn down and how many ugly little one story buildings are being put up with those ordinary plate glass fronts, and with doors stuck over to the side, and all the strange-looking people on the street, not a soul I knew by sight and remembering when I would at least be able to nod to someone on every block.

I had told Mr. Ramsey I would be in to look at hats between two-thirty and three and he was busy when I went in but didn't keep me sitting but a few minutes and then he started having his girls bring out hats and try them on, nothing I would have worn. I showed him my flowered hat, what I had in mind, and he laughed and said yes, yes, indeed he remembered it and so did the window dresser and he knew that was what I had been wanting and that was what he was saving to show me. Then with a great to-do he had one of the girls go back to the shipping department and bring in a box that hadn't yet been opened. He took it himself and cut the cord and unwrapped the parcel in such a way as to save the foreign-looking stamps and labels, and opened it up and brought it out from the tissue. Well!

Well, I wish you could have seen it, it really was beautiful, and I laughed and said Oh, Mr. Ramsey, it is lovely, but I'm twenty years too late for it. Maybe one of my daughters in a few years. And he said not at all not at all and wouldn't I try it on. I said just to see how it sits. Which of course was a mistake.

Mr. Ramsey has no sense of style. He tilted it down over one eye and I looked a fool and a hundred years old. And I said, oh, no, Mr. Ramsey, it is lovely but it won't do. But then I set it flat on my head, the line cutting straight across my brow and there was nothing frivolous about it. It was quite distinguished. Almost severe in spite of all the flowers, which weren't, I'm glad to say, gaudy. Sweet flowers, violets, and rose buds and small white and yellow flowers, so close one couldn't see the straw, not even at the edge of the broad brim. I must say it was most distinctive and I knew I could never wear my old one again after seeing such a creation.

Mr. Ramsey said he thought it was really aristocratic looking and I said I could not help agreeing but still it was too young for me. And he just kept saying no, no, and the girls kept saying no, no in a way that convinced me, I could see the admiration in their eyes, and they called in another girl who said it could not be more becoming and by then I had an idea I would take it, if I could afford it.

"It was your money," my father said. "Saved for how long?"

I didn't think I had enough money even with all I had saved, and I really hadn't meant to spend but half of it on a hat. I could see the London label and Mr. Ramsey was talking about the French woman who lived on the next block down, in the Mayberry Smith house, who trimmed hats and who could take off a bow which really was excessive and maybe she could fill it in with one of the extra flowers, you know how they send extra flowers with those hats. And I thought what all we really needed, but how I had promised myself a hat and hadn't had one in a dozen years and so I said: all right, I'll take it if it can all be done today. He telephoned the French woman while I waited and she said she could do it that afternoon if I brought it in before four o'clock and I said in that case I'd take it along and he could send my old hat today with my other packages. It even depressed me to put back on that black cloche.

"Madame Rosay," my father said.

"What?" my mother asked as if he were calling her names.

"The French lady. Her name is Madame Rosay. That's who Mr. Ramsey put me in touch with last night. When I talked to her she said you never got there."

"I didn't," my mother said.

She sipped some tea and buttered a corner of toast and looked at him as if for the first time in a year. They seldom looked directly at each other and when they did there was always a moment of silence in which the children felt left out of some secret. "I had no idea I would be so late. So really late. You must have been . . . in any case, I'm glad I wasn't here to see you."

He nodded as if she understood and had even seen him pacing the house, driving in and out the drive, and telephoning, telephoning.

"But I did keep trying to telephone home. Every chance when their backs were turned. But the line stayed busy. . . ."

"I was phoning everyone I knew and finally the police . . . ."

"It's all right," she said, glancing about the table at each of us. "No one need know he called the police except if one of you should tell and you've given me your promise. . . ."

"I don't see why you're so sensitive about your feelings when your own children went to bed not knowing whether you were alive or buried somewhere in a shallow grave by those yardmen you hire."

"Don't mention graves to me," my mother said, and then as if she were determined to be cheerful said, "It was really the only other hat I've ever seen that looked better on me and made me feel so young."

Then she went on: I started out of the store with it, thinking I'd not put it back in the box since I was only going a few doors down. At first I didn't notice there were a few drops of rain, and I was holding it in my hands like a cake, and I thought it's only a step and there are awnings halfway there. But then the drops seemed heavier and without looking I thought it was the Mayberry Smith house already and I would just duck out from under the awnings and straight up the steps to the porch and that's what I did.

A young girl, not more than fifteen, met me at the door the second I set foot on the porch and said, "Oh, you've come to see Grandmother." She took my hat and naturally I assumed I was at the right place and turned my hat over to her and she said, "It's beautiful," and then she said, "Won't you come in and speak to Mother." Very good, plain country manners. You know when we moved to town my mother said we'd never see lovely manners such as those we were leaving, but here this girl had just that nice, plain air about her and showing me into the parlor as if I were the grandest sort of company instead of someone coming to have a hat trimmed.

Well, I looked about and realized I was not in the May-berry Smith house and then it took me only one minute to realize what was going on. The whole family was arranged in chairs and sofas along the walls, all dressed in the best black they could scrape together, and a woman about my age stood up, and all the men stood up, and the girl handed the woman my hat and said, "It's for Grandmother."

"Oh!" The woman said, choking up immediately. "How unusual. How perfectly beautiful. Won't you come and see her?"

Whether I wanted to or not, she took my elbow on one side, and a young man took me by the elbow on the other and they steered me through an archway to the coffin, and there lay a perfect stranger, a woman I'd never seen in my life. I wanted to turn and run, but then I thought, no, I'm not so busy that I can't spare a few minutes to be decent. There were one or two timid-looking relatives in that room, and the mother said: "Let's place it here," and they put my hat on the coffin. There were one or two pitiful sprays there, one of carnations with a sleazy satin bow, and one home-made one with early forsythia and a sort of white flower I haven't seen since I was a girl which would have been nice if they'd left off the rayon ribbons. And then my hat. Well, I thought, I'll sit long enough to show my respect and then when I leave I'll just go put the hat on and thank them. But then I touched my forehead and realized I had on my black cloche and then's when the tears came to my eyes. They saw the tears and started making a fuss over the hat, calling it a wreath, and trying to distract me out of politeness, and saying how it put the live flowers to shame and certainly Grandmother would be proud.

The woman my age introduced herself as Anita Dobson and then introduced all of them to me and I kept looking at the old lady in the coffin and wanting to cry, the situation I'd got myself in. But Mrs. Dobson was saying: "Where did you know her?"

I thought I'd say I used to stop and chat with her on the porch but the truth was I couldn't remember ever seeing anyone on any porch on that part of Main Street, and now I wasn't even sure which house I was in, who had ever lived here, it all seemed so turned around. And I thought, well, it never does any harm to mention church and so I said, "Church." After that there was no way out.

"I knew it," Anita said, "one of Mama's Sunday School girls."

I nodded and the tears must have been coming down my

cheeks then because she offered me her handkerchief and I nodded no and took out mine and when she put her arm around me we stood there and had a good cry. Just a real good cry. Six years of savings gone.

"Oh," the young girl said, "you're the only one of them who has come and we were hoping at least one of them would."

And Mrs. Dobson said, "But it's been so many years since she was able to teach we didn't really think any of them would remember her."

I said, "I don't think I'll ever forget her." And I don't think I will.

While we sat there, waiting, I know now for the undertakers (the Mauldin Brothers, wouldn't you know they'd have the Mauldins) I learned that it was a Mrs. Ralph Carruthers who was dead and that she was eighty-four and they were, just as I suspected, from up-country, not far from my own grandmother's place, and that they hadn't lived in town long enough for the old lady to make any friends of her own and that not many of them knew many people here and that they hoped more would be at the church and that I certainly would come along to the church with them, wouldn't I?

I couldn't very well ask what church and by that time the hearse was there and the Mauldin brothers and men folks were rolling the coffin through the living room and before I had time to stand up and say "My hat," they were already going across the front porch with it, and down those side steps.

I thought, well, it wouldn't do me any harm to go to church every now and then, and I wouldn't be much farther from home than now no matter which church in town. There's not one I couldn't walk home from and I said, yes, I intended going to the church but that I had wanted to stop by and pay my respects first. They all were kissing me again and saying I must ride with the family, they had engaged two cars but they had other cars, cousins and such and in any case, they wanted me to sit in the front car with the family, and so there I marched out with them, straightening my gloves and dabbing at my eyes, as if I were one of them. They must never find out.

My mother glanced about the table at us and at my father who was grinning so proudly at her he looked drunk.

So, off we went! The hearse moving out and then us and cars stopping and the policemen directing us through the traffic lights, and everything else but us coming to a complete halt, and between the shoulders of the Mauldin sons I could see the hearse up ahead with the two sprays and my hat and it was one of the saddest thoughts in the world that a woman could die with no more recognition than that and

I almost decided I wouldn't try to get the hat back at the end of the service.

First I thought, because we were going up Kirkpatrick Street that it would be at the A.R.P. Presbyterian Church, and then when they drove past that I thought, it's going to be the St. Paul's Methodist out on Betts Place, and when we drove on past Betts Place without turning I knew I would have to telephone your office and ask you to send for me. It had quit raining for a spell now and then I realized we were going faster than a funeral procession should, we were in the outskirts then, past all those used-car places, and it was open country on each side and I didn't know how to phrase it, but I finally said: "Oh, you're going to the *old* church."

Mrs. Dobson said yes. And the granddaughter said that that was where the old lady wanted to be buried from, where she'd married: "Ebeneezer." You know there's an Ebeneezer on every country road in South Carolina and I didn't have sense enough to be worried.

We drove and we drove and we drove. It seemed to me an hour at least and then the man in the hearse stopped, in the middle of open country, and signalled, and our driver went up and talked to him and came back and reported very respectfully he would stop in Tryon, North Carolina. He was having trouble with his windshield wipers and didn't want to be driving on mountain roads without them. Tryon!

There was a phone in the garage. That's the first time I called. It was already after five o'clock and not an answer at your office and of course this line was busy.

So there was nothing to do but get back in and in a way I'm glad I did. (The service was planned for six o'clock and the Mauldin brothers apologized for driving so fast but all arrangements had been made for the church and we mustn't be late.) It was one of the finest sermons I've heard preached. They just don't preach like that anymore, I imagine. It was good, honest, country preaching. For awhile I thought he was going to be one of those men who would shout too much but he kept his voice just inside breaking. And I sat there with the family, and I'm glad because there weren't more than a handful of people in the church, each coming up with a little handful of homegrown flowers, in fruit jars wrapped in tinfoil, and all of them seeming a bit shy as they placed them next to my hat. It made me ashamed. What the preacher said made me ashamed of feeling so possessive and materialistic. (I kept thinking, even if I don't get it back at the graveside, it's been put to good use.) Vanity, vanity.

At the end of the service Mrs. Dobson said, "You will go to the graveyard with us." Well, naturally I thought she meant the one right outside, or the new part across the road in the cedar grove, and I said, "Yes." I didn't have any way of leaving anyway. The rented family cars and the Mauldin brothers had gone back during the hour-long service and the men in the hearse were the only ones going on.

So we all crowded into one of the old cars parked there and still thinking we might just be going to the back of the cedar grove I didn't mind being crowded.

But the hearse pulled out and we pulled out, the rain still spattering, and headed straight toward the mountains. "Where is she to be buried?" I asked.

"At her home place. There's a family graveyard there," the granddaughter answered. Mrs. Dobson was crying again.

"Her home place," I wept. "Yes. She loved it so much."

Mrs. Dobson put her hand over mine and squeezed it but I still had no idea we were going all the way across the Tennessee state line till I saw a sign saying: "Rock City, Tennessee." I knew then I wouldn't be home before midnight and so I said I simply would need to stop and make a call and that's when I called the second time and the line was still busy here so I called Mrs. Honeycutt's sister.

"Why didn't you call one of the neighbors?"

"And have the whole neighborhood know I was way up in Tennessee without your father? It already dark. What could they have thought?"

"She didn't get the message to us until ten o'clock," my father said.

"By ten o'clock we already had the body in the living room of the Carrutherses' old house," my mother said. The grave was already open but they weren't going to bury her until sunrise. There was to be a sitting-up, but the men in the hearse said they were coming back and I asked if I could ride with them. I got in and we drove back to put a canvas over the open grave and in the headlights of the hearse I could see what those men had done. They'd planted all those little jars of flowers in the red mud piled up by the grave, and there at the head, in the pouring down rain, was my hat stuck up on one of those tacky little stands they use for wreaths.

"Why did you?" I asked the driver. He wanted to know what and I said, "Why did you put the flowers at the grave?"

"That's our job, lady," he said. "What we're paid to do."

He dropped a pebble in the grave and listened to it splash while I stared at the ruined flowers on the hat. (No one else had noticed my hat gone any more than I had, we were all so concerned about getting the body across the rotten porch and getting chairs arranged, and eating all the food the neighbors had brought.) I asked the driver if I could ride in back, knowing I'd feel safer back there than I would sitting up front with two strange men. The other man walked me under the umbrella to the back of the hearse, opened the door just as polite as you please, and said, before shutting the door, "Pleasant dreams, lady!"

"And did you have?" my father asked.

"It was one of the most comfortable rides I've ever had. I slept the entire way. The first thing I knew we were parked in front of the house and you were opening the door and it was almost morning. I want you to promise me one thing: when I die. . . ."

"For God's sake!" my father set his coffee cup down with a clatter, threw his napkin on the table, and stood, "Don't even talk about it. It was bad enough . . . waiting . . . seeing you brought home in a hearse. . . ."

I'd never seen tears in my father's eyes before and I'd never seen my mother leave a table without saying a word, but before he reached the bottom step she had her hand on his elbow. I can not remember ever seeing them touch each other but that one morning as they walked up the stairs, his arm around her waist, her bare head on his shoulder.

The Girl from Carthage

HE HAD telephoned the night before and asked her if he could bring the children back before lunch instead of after. He had not said why and she had not asked. No one had told her he was going to marry again, but in their prescient ways which had made their marriage both exciting and impossible, she knew. Signs from him and from the way his mother changed the subject when his name came up casually now at lunches. She had been certain when he said: "I wrote you a note, did you get it?" She had not been down to the mailbox, and now she was so certain that she didn't need to go. It would be short and direct and every sentence would begin: "Edwina."

It was funny but she wanted to be wearing a dress when she saw him even though he liked her best in slacks. When she heard the car, she came out in an antelope-colored shirt-dress, and no one could be sure without touching it whether it was thick silk or purest chamois. Standing in the parking area he did not touch it or her, though she felt the tension of his not touching her. They talked for awhile about the new gate, the last thing he had installed for them: a country wooden Z gate with chain and padlock, and the surprising thing was that the entire gate, chain and post, swung open at the sound of his or her car horn. It had taken five men from his factory two days to work out the design: both the gate and the post swinging open, leaving the electric fence to protect the rest of the frontage. It bordered on cute and she dreaded hearing Lib Anderson saying it was amusing; but now with the character of Pinehurst changing so fast it was probably a sensible thing for him to do.

"I will feel safer," he was saying. "Strangers aren't likely to guess anyway that there's a house back here."

"You sound as if you're going away," she said, knowing he needed help in telling her. He had appreciated her cue and had told her then he was marrying, a girl she didn't know, someone he'd met in New York. No, he didn't have time for a drink which she thought would be nice.

"I would have mentioned it earlier but I assumed you'd guessed."

"I gathered," she said, and as though it were her dress she had gathered, she plunged her hands into the deep side-vent pockets at each hip, thankful they were there. The dress though was a mistake. It was too hot for the day. She had learned to spend money, but not enough. He would know it was an end-of-the-season sale. A markdown. She envied his ease with clothes: the unironed denim shirt, the starched khakis. She always felt overdressed around him. His first and main criticism of her had been: "You're so damned self-conscious about everything." And his final, irretrievable criticism had been: "You're so damned self-conscious I can't make love to you." They had been lying on top of the tan velvet cover which they hadn't turned back, and he had gotten up and dressed and in her memory walked from there right on out of the house though of course there had been weeks in between.

Looking at the stone wing of the house, the old gristmill part, he put his arm on her shoulder, pulled her easily to him and kissed her ear. He let his hand stay on her shoulder and said, apparently at the touch of the suede: "We do need to go over some bills. I don't think they gave you credit for Allen's coat."

"I didn't send it back," she said. Before he could question her she added: "It will fit Toby in a year or so."

She saw it go through his mind how fast moths get into camel's hair and then the thing that really troubled him: how fast his sons were growing. "Is it worth keeping it?"

"Some things are worth keeping. If they can't be replaced." She hated all their words having other meanings.

"You're echoing," he said. "That's my line."

He was talking about furniture again. He had moved his mother's French antiques out of the house, furnished his apartment, stored other things, and she had filled in the bare spaces with really good contemporary furniture and a few pieces of North Carolina primitives, all of which would become antiques. When he asked her she had said yes she was that sure of her taste, they would become more valuable every year.

She had always been sure of her own taste and last month when her friends, his friends really, said, "No one but you could have gotten away with purple walls," she knew they weren't sure whether she had or not. Her secret joke was that she hadn't. They were too purple for a library, nothing you could relax with, or forget. She'd intended a much greyer purple, a softer light, aged, faded.

"Do you have then just a minute," she asked. He would be flattered and amused. "I need help. Desperately." They walked around the house to the terrace door that opened directly into the library. She pointed to the walls and laughed. She knew he would be kind as he inevitably was since he had moved out. As, in fairness, was his nature.

"They almost work," he said. "I imagine with the curtains drawn they do." He looked about. "I imagine it's nice at night." They had always agreed the room was too large and needed to be made smaller. The Chinese screens had made it larger and junky instead of smaller. "Isn't it good at night?"

"Not really," she said.

"Glaze them. Get Clarence to use a silver glaze, it'll put a bloom on them, like on a plum, but it'll take away some of the red."

"It is the red that's wrong, isn't it?"

"Maybe even a bronze glaze, if you want to go toward brown. But it might get muddy. I'd say silver."

They were both excited. "I won't have to have it painted over?"

"I'd try a light glaze first. Get Clarence to try over in the corner. Behind the chair. You'll have to watch him, he'll want to overdo it and it'll end up like an aluminum beer can." There was a terrible silence in which she thought she heard her pocket watch ticking on the table. Here they were at their closest and best. If they hadn't finished the house and landscaping they would still be together. Still waking up in the middle of the night and making out lists of projects which each would do with astonishing efficiency, eating quick lunches, walking about the place talking to workmen as they ate. She wanted now to ask if he would call Clarence and explain to him exactly, but now with mention of the marriage she couldn't. It was her pulse, not the watch on the table. Outside the children were feeling at home again and beginning to talk too loud about something. In the library they both looked at each other embarrassed and both hurried out the French doors to the sunlight on the terrace.

FOR AWHILE after he drove through the outer gate the crunch of the gravel stayed in her ears as if it were the river. Something was definitely wrong with her ears. She felt lately that they held on to sounds too long; and her eyes too seemed slow to release images. She lived in a world of echo and montage. P. B. Jones had reassured her there were no symptoms of brain tumor. Still, she thought, maybe she should go up to Duke, consult a specialist. The effect, though, of these sensual memories was rather pleasant, like good pot fantasies. The only trouble was she wanted to be alone to enjoy the sensations and how could you with one nine-year-old boy and one five? Now she was hearing the car door slam again. Was it one of her echoes or had he stopped to check the electronic thing on the gate? Or the mailbox to see if his note had come the day before?

"Daddy's going to get married," Toby was saying. She looked to see if he had really said what she heard but Toby was working on the iron step-rail with a new screwdriver, apparently a gift from his father, the thing he would play with and sleep with all week. The dream feeling was going on too long. Had he been given a screwdriver the week before and the week before that too? It was all too familiar. She asked him what he had said and he said again: "Daddy's going to get married."

Allen who was suddenly with them said: "Toby, we weren't

supposed to be listening." He turned to his mother and said: "Daddy told Agatha last night after he talked to you."

"Agatha?" she asked as if she did not recognize the name.

"Grandmother," Allen said. "She said I could call her Agatha the way you and Daddy do."

"I think 'Grandmother' would be nicer." Then she realized maybe the woman did not want to be reminded of her age, looking as remarkably young as she did. "But whatever she says."

"But he is going to get married again," Toby was telling them and himself.

"How nice for him." She was pleased with her tone. If she had to hear the news, it was good to hear it first from Dan and then from her own son. Of course Dan would naturally be courteous enough to let her be the third person to know, even if it was simply so she could help the children understand.

On the front lawn the sheep were slowly cropping the grass in the shade of the elm. Far down below, the river was echoing the gravel crunch. "Every leaf seems always perfectly in place," she could hear Lib Anderson and a dozen other women say. She didn't trust these alien women who admired her poise and the composure of her house in their hoarse Northern voices. She didn't want the place to be so obvious and planned. They might interpret it as fright. That's why she had insisted on incorporating the old gristmill into the design of the house. She wanted to declare: "I'm from Carthage, North Carolina, and I feel at home here."

She told the boys she had found their turtle, up near the boulder in the apple orchard, and walked with them across the cobblestone parking area to the gate of the kitchen garden. When they were almost out of sight, running up the hill to the boulder, she turned and walked down the sweep of the drive. From the lawn below the drive she could see the house as it had been photographed for *Architectural Statements*: three immense slabs of stone, like steps, with glass rooms and slate roofs on each, leading up to a strange stone structure which was the shell of the old gristmill or armory left from the Civil War. No one really knew exactly what it had been built for. It was three stories high and had strange double wooden doors and openings placed oddly but now glassed in. The magazine writer had praised it for the way it had been integrated with the contemporary part and how it had all been made to seem an organic feature of the hillside. To her, at the moment, it looked damned crazy. Schizophrenic. And who would ever buy it?

She went back through the gate of the kitchen garden and stood among the herbs studying the rock walls and feeling homesick for the place in Normandy where they had gone the first two summers of their marriage. The dreamlike feeling was persisting uncomfortably long. Everything was in slow motion, the sheep cropping, the apple trees rustling, even their voices, Allen's and Toby's from beyond the old tennis court. She stood very still waiting for the world to start moving at regular speed again. She could see herself breaking the moment by rushing into the house, letting her dull blonde hair fall down to her waist and chopping it off with the kitchen shears.

No, she would do none of those dikey things some women did soon after divorce. No tailored pantsuits, boots, short hair. Nor would she go frilly, fussy, girlish again. Maybe one light streak in her hair, which she had neglected to do since their separation. But nothing entirely new and different.

Again she could feel her pulse beating in her ears. Even knowing all along, she was still surprised. Certainly he would marry again. Certainly she would. They were both far more attractive than they had been twelve years ago. Still she was angry, jealous, sad, offended. Not even three weeks after the final papers. Later, alone, she would sort out her feelings. At the moment she felt stupid and incapable standing there in the chamois dress she knew he would like. She needed to be alone for several hours and then everything would find its place. But with Louise back in France for Easter who would stay with the children while she drove over the familiar back country roads?

Allen, sensing something strange, was standing at the gate watching her. "He's telling the truth," Allen said. Allen saw himself apparently as the family historian. It was his self-appointed task to keep all records, especially Toby's, straight.

"Well," she said, "well well." As if she were talking about or to the butterfly on the white lilac. The lilac bush had always been in the wrong place. It should have been planted down near the road gate, way off to one side of it. There was no way to be unself-conscious about lilacs and elms. Unless you sort of threw them away. Butterflies, hummingbirds, and bluebirds too. She would trade them all for one good chicken hawk, or at the moment, for a frizzled hen. It had been years since she'd seen a frizzled chicken. She turned to Allen: "Did you ever see a frizzled hen?"

He asked what and she repeated the question, not sure she had asked it before, and then Toby asked What and she repeated it all again, bored with the subject before she got through with the explanation. "A chicken with its feathers growing the wrong way. They look like they're standing with their backs to a strong wind." "Their tails to a gale," her father had always said when they rode out through the country to visit a sick parishioner. She was homesick, that was it. Enough to chop off her hair to be a frizzled chicken.

"Why do they stand with their backs to the wind?" Toby asked.

"They don't, stupid," Allen said, nine, wise, going on ten. "Their feathers grow that way."

"I want to see one," Toby said.

"So do I, darling," Edwina said. But she could not afford to go soft. "Did Daddy give you your allowance?"

Toby showed her the screwdriver he'd bought and Allen showed her three quarters. He was saving to buy a kit of magic tricks.

Overhead the cumulus was building and over the river they stretched in one direction toward Pinehurst and in the other toward Carthage. Once lightning had struck the steeple of the little Episcopal church where her father usually preached but that Sunday he'd been at the university and his absence gave him more prestige than his presence ever had. The sky was dark over Carthage now and a rain cloud was moving fast down the valley. The rumbling thunder was like the boards on the covered bridge when they passed over in the Studebaker. There was something wrong with her time-sense. She wished she'd asked P. B. whether smoking pot was dangerous for some people. Instead of all those questions about brain tumors. He'd surprised her by asking her as though it was the most relevant thing in the world: "How old are you?"

"I'm forty," she had said. "I look forty, I feel forty, and I am forty."

P. B., the bastard, had said, "No woman is ever forty." He had claimed all women were thirty-nine for two years and then when they were almost forty-two they became forty.

She walked through the gusty breeze across the cobblestones and around to the front lawn that sloped to the meadow. In the large sheets of glass she could see the clouds and then the trees, the sheep, and then herself walking up the little slope to the house. Even when he knew his jealousy of the architect was unreasonable, he had not quit being jealous of the house. "It's so completely narcissistic," had been his only real but repeated complaint. "You're trying to make it an extension of yourself."

"I know who I am," she said. "I've always known."

"Take all your objects away from you," he said, "and you have no idea."

"Move me a thousand miles in my sleep," she said, "and I can replace them all with others just as good, better."

"And you would, too," he said. "You need mirrors. You don't exist without them. Every object has to be you."

Now at the door she touched her fingertips to the image in the door and adjusted the bun at the nape of her neck.

She had argued that all her artifacts were romantic, sentimental, reminders of those people she had admired and thus
learned from, consciously copied. Her blonde hair parted in
the middle and drawn loosely back to the heavy bun: had he
looked recently at the portrait of his own grandmother, the
one picture she coveted in his mother's house? Could it be,
she argued, that she was simply a mirror of everyone she had
admired? Didn't that explain her spectacular career; his
grandfather's secretary at the mill, then personnel manager
of the new dress line, then head of the advertising in the
New York office, and finally bride of the grandson. No one
had ever called her ambitious because she had never been
ambitious. "I simply knew when I was four years old and
almost everything in sight was ugly that someday everything
I had would be beautiful. He had actually blushed when she
added: "And you are."

He'd said, "But someday I intend to be fat and bald" and
she said no she simply would not allow it and had given him
lettuce for lunch.

She paused a moment before going into the house. She
was not beautiful, she knew that, but she gave the impression of being lovely, she had been told often enough. If it
were true, it was because of her practiced calmness, serenity,
the modulation of her low voice and laugh. "All American
women touch their faces in public," his English grandmother

had taught her, "and it is a most unattractive habit." She had acquired all she could in the way of poise by watching his grandmother and mother. And from every woman she knew and admired. Sometimes she knew that if she had started with more assurance, she would have become a great lover of women, even a lesbian, in her constant search for teachers.

His final words before he moved out had been a rebuke to her but true. "I want ugly things around me," he said. "Women so ugly I'll get warts from touching them."

Sympathy in his family had been for her, and because she had wanted to keep nothing they insisted on her taking everything they had ever given her. It was at a recent lunch with his mother and grandmother that she'd left at her place at the table the jewelry they'd given her, tied in tissue with a loose ribbon. But when she got in the car to drive off there it was on the driver's seat. It was not mentioned then or ever.

"You pooh-pooh Mama." Toby was screaming from the dining room. She took off her shoes and walked across the living room and holding on to the rail looked down into the dining room. "You pooh-pooh pee-pee, yucky old Mama!" He was furious.

"Toby," she said.

"I hate you doo-doo woman." He stared up at her not yet crying.

"Toby, what have *I* done?"

"Wrecked my castle." He had crawled under the monastery table.

"Toby, I asked you to move it before you left. In the first place I've asked you not to play on that rug."

"I hate this pee-pee rug. I'm going to cut it up with a butcher knife. I'm going to get an ax. . . ."

She walked down the steps toward him and sat on the bottom one. Through the pantry doors she could see Allen rolling a green tennis ball down the butcher-block table toward a heavy glass vase. "Allen," she called, "not near the vase."

"I'm being careful," he said, but his voice held more anger than Toby's. "Toby called Grandmother pooh-pooh at breakfast yesterday."

"I don't like tattling," she said.

"He's a goddamned tattler," Toby said.

She gave him again her lecture on bad words and made him come and look her directly in the eye while she spoke. "Mainly, I'm just tired of all your silly, baby words: pooh-pooh, pee-pee, goddamn this and that, doo-doo, ca-ca, they're all so babyish. I don't want you and Allen to sound like babies. People might make fun of you."

"They're not baby," Toby said without conviction. "They're dirty nasty words."

"Oh my," she said with pity, "are those the dirtiest words you know?"

"I know peter and dick," he said.

"That's not very dirty," she said. "Babies know those words." Allen started up the steps from the pantry. "He says ass and butt."

"Ass and butt," she repeated. "All baby words. I wish you knew some really dirty words," she said, "not baby words."

Allen was drawing nearer, puzzled. "But ass is a dirty word, isn't it?"

"Oh, it's not a pretty word, but I wouldn't call it dirty."

Toby was touching her now, his anger spent. "Do you know any dirty words?" he asked.

"Hundreds of them," she said. Curiously, "ambitious" was the first word that came to her.

"What ones?" Toby asked.

"All of them," she said. "In French and in English."

Allen was staring at her as incredulously as Toby. "Do you, Mother?"

"Certainly. That's why I get so bored with you and with Toby when you get angry and talk all that baby talk."

"Where did you learn French ones?" Allen asked.

"In France. And from Louise."

"Louise?" Allen clearly could not believe that the live-in student talked dirty.

"After she's put you and Toby to bed."

"What words? What words do you know?"

"Well, I certainly can't tell you." She stood up and walked to the window. Cloud shadows were gliding over the meadow and on the distant hill a huge cumulo-nimbus was flashing from its dark center. The paper had had a story on the possibility of the young peach crop being ruined by hailstorms. "Maybe we should put those plywood sheets over the greenhouse," she said.

"Where did you learn them, the English ones," Allen asked.

"Will you help me? We can put a canvas over the plywood."

"The dirty words," Allen persisted.

She went out the side door and through the kitchen garden and the three of them slid the plywood onto the roof of the greenhouse and weighted it down with some Chinese tiles they'd never found a place for. All the time Toby was saying he bet ca-ca asshole was dirtier then any word she knew, French or English.

Back in the living room, iced tea in hand, she put her feet up and tried to distract them by asking questions about Agatha and the house but not about their father. But again Toby was saying, "That's not fair. You've got to tell us."

"I can't," she said, pushing his blond bangs back to show the curved top of his forehead.

"Mother, Toby's right you know. It isn't polite to start to say something and then not finish it."

"Why can't you tell us?"

"Because," she said as if that was all she intended to say but then went on, "if I did tell you, then you'd be sure to use one of them and I'd be so shocked I'd have to go straight up to my room and stay locked up in there all day."

"Like when you have a headache?" Toby asked.

"Or when you're smoking?" Allen asked.

The idea of being locked in her own room all afternoon was so immensely pleasing to her she began planning immediately what she would want to have with her. A pitcher of tea, tuna fish salad, toasted saltines left from breakfast, the new unopened magazines, the wildflower catalogue, the seashells that had arrived Wednesday from New Zealand. A magnifying glass. And after it all, after a shower on the flat roof, and maybe a nap, she would ease her mind and think rationally about his marrying again. "No," she said, "I couldn't possibly trust you not to repeat them."

In the kitchen they begged her while she set out their lunches and made her tray ready.

"We won't ever say them."

"I don't use the ones I know," Allen said. "Some I've never told even you or Daddy."

"I haven't either," Toby said. "Just one. One little old dirty one."

"Just one, Mother."

"But think how I would feel if you repeated it and I had to go lock myself in my room all afternoon in embarrassment." Her tray was really handsome enough to be photographed and she kept adding a few things she was discovering in the refrigerator: marmalades she had forgotten, watermelon pickles.

Heavy rain was splashing on the panes and a nice comfortable thunder was rumbling down the valley.

"A really bad awful dirty word."

She picked up her tray and walked up the steps and across the dining room and up the steps to the living room. She sat again and said, "Promise."

They promised so sincerely and solemnly she wanted to kiss them. But then she was at a complete loss for a word. Finally it came to her, and she said it slowly, louder than a whisper, but still confidentially: "Manipulate."

It sounded as awful to her as it did when she first came across it in her father's church library. He'd left the bookcase on marriage counseling unlocked and in a book by Havelock Ellis she had discovered an ominous sentence, malignant in its horror: "Indeed, manipulation of self could be considered by some to be the preferred sexual stimulation of the person with strong and admitted narcissistic traits." Every word, until she had looked them up, furtively, one by one, in her father's dictionary had seemed to be almost tangibly dirty.

She allowed each of them to say the word once and then sent them off to put away their clothes. She carried a pitcher of tea and the little wooden crate of seashells to her room on the level above and had come back down to watch the rain on the kitchen garden when she heard them slamming the doors to the bathroom between their rooms. Now they were in the hall, shouting, furious, each claiming the sailboat. And then it came, Toby's voice: "You goddamn old manipulate."

"Toby! Mother! . . ."

"I heard," she said. She marched straight up to the dining room, and then up to the living room with them following, and then up to her room where, in spite of their pleas and promises and apologies, she locked the door, as soon as she'd set down the beautiful tray.

Later, after a long dream in which a man dressed like a priest had been speaking French to her in a patois she could not quite understand, she opened her eyes and was surprised there was still light in the sky. A strong, almost cold breeze was lifting the curtains on the doors that led to the deck on the gristmill roof. It was a little after sunset, she gathered, and down below she could hear Allen with his guitar singing to Toby about the magic dragon. The long bath, the nap were all she'd needed, really—to be alone for awhile and not have to entertain the children while trying to think about him. There was nothing actually to think she hadn't thought about a year before. With a complacency which surprised her she recombed her hair, put on a velvet robe, exactly warm enough, and went down to the kitchen where they were sitting. After supper she would make up her behavior to them by making fudge and reading a long story to them and it would be a day like any other day.

Allen stopped singing when he saw her but she insisted he go on. She sliced the cold roast and made rice and poured the milk and acted as if it were the most ordinary day in her life. As they sat eating at the butcher-block table, using paper towels for napkins which she had forgot to buy, there was the silence she had expected, and then Allen had said he was sorry for what had happened and Toby had said he was sorry and then Allen had said: "But can I ask you one thing, Mother?"

"If it won't shock me," she said.

"Then maybe I'd better not ask."

"Oh, go ahead. It's not polite to stop halfway through you know." She could not remember having told him that and wondered who he had picked it up from.

"What does it mean?"

At first she thought he meant what did it mean that Dan was remarrying, but then he said, "That word: *manipulate*."

"It means," she said (she had no intention of telling him what it had meant to her that dreadful afternoon when she discovered the name of the deed), "it means a way of using people without their knowing they're being used." She looked up into the dining room where the Chinese rug was folded thickly back against the leg of the sixteenth century monastery table. "To get what you want." She had not known that her breathing and her voice would play tricks on her, but she managed to finish: "Even if you don't want anything and you thought all along you did."

"Like my other green tennis ball," Allen said.

"I don't think that's very dirty." Toby was disappointed.

"It might make a person feel dirty though, mightn't it, Mother?" Allen asked. But then in the same tone he asked if she knew where the other green tennis ball was. "You said leave them here and they wouldn't get lost."

She remembered telling him that before he got in the car, and she remembered taking them from him and bringing them to the kitchen. But she remembered too that had been a year ago at least. Again everything seemed far away and in slow-motion and the last raindrops were echoing on the cobblestones.

"Mama, if you were a frizzled hen would Allen and I be frizzled too?"

She had known he was going to ask that and she knew before he said it that now he would say: "Is frizzled a dirty word?"

"If you'd asked me yesterday, I would have said 'yes'." But before they could ponder on a word being dirty one day and not the next she remembered and said: "Allen, look in the vase. You were rolling the ball toward it this morning."

"And that's where it is." He reached into the thick vase and pulled out the lost ball. She watched him studying it and thought again about what he'd said: one might feel dirty by manipulating people to get what one wanted.

But who, after all, had she manipulated and compromised more than herself—all to please a man and his family. Her father's favorite sermon had always been about the man who gained the entire world and lost his own soul. Had it ever occurred to him to preach about a woman giving up the entire world to gain a man? Or a woman giving up a man to regain her own soul? But again she looked about, up the steps into the dining room, and wondered who would ever buy such a crazy, four-level house.

"I still want to see a frizzled chicken," Toby was saying.

"We'll go tomorrow to look for one," she said, and to herself added: "To hell with the Day School."

"Where?"

"On the back roads."

"Pinehurst?"

"Carthage. They're found only in the poorest people's yards. They take dust baths under those houses that stand up off the ground with no shrubbery."

"They bathe under the houses?" Toby was delighted.

But Allen understood: "The chickens, stupid. Not the people."

"Why do they?" Toby asked.

"Maybe it's cooler under there," she said. "And I'll show you where your grandmother was born."

"Agatha?" Allen asked.

"No. Where my mother was born." She could see the ugly old Victorian house, grey and sagging, with the porch running around three sides. She could see the porch swing and the ferns and sitting in a cane rocking chair a young girl stringing beans into a chipped enamel pan. An honest, straightforward plain girl with straight blonde hair and a few summer freckles.

She did not know how long she contemplated the honest, unaffected girl on the porch, but long enough to fall in love with her; and it was from far off, beyond the pecan trees, that she heard Allen saying: "Why are you crying, Mother?"

She bent her head until the butcher-block table was cutting across her forehead. Her father always said, "All tears are tears of self-pity." But he was wrong. There could be tears of homecoming, tears of joy. She wondered how many divorced women felt them without knowing what they were.

The Glass-Brick Apartment

THEY TELL me here that it sometimes helps to remember events accurately and to see them all again. I was ten the summer my Uncle Nat was taken away sick and I was not to talk about it with any of the neighbors.

Four years before that summer when I came to live with my grandparents, Uncle Nat had moved out of his upstairs room to the basement where he'd made a cool, dry apartment for himself. It was the time in the early thirties when everything was Modern—meaning, in the South, glass-brick. Uncle Nat, by saving each week, had managed during two years to replace the old sunbaked bricks with glass ones. The lot sloped from the street to the creek and the apartment had full-sized windows, the sills of which were a good two feet above the garden path. Often he stood, very tall and bony, looking out the big plate glass window at the garden and the stream.

My grandmother was against the idea of the apartment from the very beginning. Uncle Frank, her oldest son, had been killed in France; Uncle Charles had left home when he was sixteen, and no one knew where he was; Fred, the youngest, my father, came only at Christmastime. Uncle Nat

49

was the only one left. Except for two years at the university, he had lived all his life in a room across from my grandmother's. The room had a high ceiling and a ceiling fan, and one of Uncle Nat's toy airplanes still hung from the center of the fan and circled slowly when the fan was turning. He and my grandmother had fought every day for two months while he and Will Jason, a Negro who had worked for him at his florist shop before it was closed by the Depression, were wallboarding the basement.

"Living in a basement!" my grandmother seemed to say at least once every day. "If you don't come down with consumption, it'll be something worse."

I remember one day when she said it, we were in the front parlor and she was standing in the tall windows which reached from floor to ceiling, fussing with the dark red velvet drapes. Uncle Nat was standing by the door with a cup of flour he had come up to borrow.

"What's worse?" I asked, hoping for descriptions of a tropical disease so horrible I could not go to sleep.

"Living at home," Grandpa said. He loved Grandmother and Uncle Nat, but not when they were together.

"Why," I whispered to Grandpa, "is living at home worse?"

He fingered his empty pipe and glanced up through his white brows. When he winked I knew he meant: "Later, when we walk down to Five Points for the evening paper."

She had seen him wink. "Make him think of his mother." She jerked the drapes and the brass rings jumped along the brass rod. "Make him homesick."

But Grandpa and I had talked about it the first time my grandmother slapped me. He knew I was glad that my mother was keeping books for some peach growers and that I was here for the summer. I was glad that my parents were getting separation papers and that in the fall my mother and I would have a very small apartment in a large apartment house with balconies and with a policeman at the corner. My father couldn't bother us then.

"Have you written your father?" Grandmother asked. She had opened my last letter from him and knew that he didn't like living alone. She believed it when, at the end of the letter, he promised to quit drinking. She didn't know him like I did. My father had gone off to school and had married without returning. "He didn't get away soon enough," my mother used to say. "Still, he's better off than Nat." She never said why. To keep now from telling Grandmother that I had written him, I asked: "Why is Daddy better off than Uncle Nat?"

"Who told you that?" She seemed taller when she walked under the glass beads of the chandelier to the dark mantel. I looked to Grandpa for help, but he was studying his pipe.

"You see what she's been telling him?" Grandmother said.

Here, "she" meant my mother; at home, "she" meant my grandmother.

"Why do you call her 'She'?" I asked. "Don't you know her name?"

She could hear the anger in my voice. "Careful how you talk to me," she said. "You're getting a little too smart to suit me."

I hated her. At that moment when she turned and started out of the room, stiff and proud, I thought again how I wanted to take my BB gun and shoot at her in her stiff corsets.

Grandpa and Uncle Nat were watching me and I was afraid they could see what I was thinking. Uncle Nat smiled, not much, but enough to show the edges of his large, even teeth. "How do you like living in my old room?"

I told him I liked the fan and the airplane and the army-boy adventure books left over from when he was a little boy.

"He's still a little boy," Grandpa said.

Uncle Nat quit smiling. He stared at my grandfather a while before he finally said: "Like father, like son." Sometimes it was no better here than it was at home. Just when you were all set to like everybody, they didn't like each other. Uncle Nat walked out of the room and the door to his stairs clicked shut.

Grandpa shook his head. "Forty years old and still single

and still living at home." While Grandpa played with his empty pipe, I sat on the arm of his chair. When I saw that he was not going to say anything else, I asked him my question again: "Which'd you rather be run over by: an old Greyhound bus or a new one?" He still hadn't answered that one.

I REMEMBER that later that summer Uncle Nat and I were at the foot of the garden when he asked me in a funny voice: "How did your mother treat your father?"

He was sitting on an old broken-down wicker chair and wore only a pair of khaki shorts and dirty white sneakers. His skin was as brown as the hair on his chest and legs. He'd been clipping hedges but had stopped to sweat. All he did now that the florist was closed was to tend the garden, sometimes with Will Jason, but usually by himself.

I was washing marbles in a sand pool in the creek. We'd been talking about where I lived and how many rooms and things like that when he asked me that question in a funny voice.

"Sir?" I said. I didn't know how to answer. My father was my father, and mother my mother, and nobody "treated" anybody any way. "I don't know."

"It's none of my business," he said. "I shouldn't have asked."

"Grandpa says you ought to get married."

"Maybe that's why I was asking."

"You're going to marry Mother?" I glanced at him. It would be funny to have to call him "Daddy." I grinned. He looked a little like my father.

"Why're you laughing?" He frowned.

"I'd have to call you 'Uncle Daddy' then."

"I'm old enough to have a son your age." He quit frowning. "I'm old enough to have a son ready to go off to the university."

"Would he live in the basement with you?" I still hadn't been in his apartment. When I was sure he wasn't there, I would peep through the plate glass window and try to see why he kept it all locked and secret.

"What?" he asked, already way off.

He was staring across the garden and creek at the woods. I watched and listened too. The late morning sun was slanting through the water oaks and willows and lighting up the crape myrtle and the water where it foamed white around the wet green rocks. A white butterfly was flicking under the bushes and over the water and up over the rocks. A swarm of gnats hung near the moss bank and moved, the whole cloud of them, in sudden jerks, up, then settled slowly back.

"It's all got by so fast," he said. "A man thinks life is going to be. . . ."

I waited. His lips moved but I could hear only bee noises

from the crape myrtle, and from the woods beyond, noon noises, hot and still.

He looked so much like my father I felt, for the first time, kin to him; and I felt the same kind of shyness I felt when my father was happy-drunk. But when I tried to sit on the arm of his chair he jumped up. The chair fell over and landed on top of me. He did not try to lift it off, but stood over me, whispering through the wicker, as if I were a wild animal in a cage: "Don't touch me!"

I lay in the grass under the wicker chair, unhurt, but wanting to cry and not to cry. I was not stunned, but I was not breathing.

"Crazy! Crazy! All of you are crazy!" I wanted to shout as he hurried toward his apartment under the house. That's what my mother said to my father and to me, too, when I lost my temper. Instead, I said, not loud enough for him to hear: "I don't want to touch you."

I was embarrassed for him and for myself. Breathing again, no longer needing to cry or not to, I wanted only to get out from under the chair and across the stream and to sit in the dugout which my father and uncles had dug when they were young.

My grandmother had seen it all, just as she saw everything. Already she was rapping on his window, and, not seeing him, was coming down the garden path toward where I lay under the chair. As she stepped through the flower border and onto the grass, she called to me: "What did you do to him?"

"What?" I asked, standing up with the chair between her and me.

"Don't you say 'what' to me!"

"Ma'am?" I asked.

"What did you put on him?" She studied the chair as though she expected to see a snake or a lizard or a tadpole. I could not tell her that I had merely wanted to put my hand on his shoulder, that sitting there he looked sad and like my father. I could tell her nothing.

"You're more trouble," she said, "than all my four sons put together."

I wanted to say, "You go to hell." But I just stood there, out of her reach, and let her stare at me and I stared right back into her grey eyes without blinking. I pressed my lips together tight to let her know how much I hated her and how much I wished she were dead. We stared without moving.

Behind me I could see the water white against the stones and could see again the white butterfly skimming the water, but all the time I was staring into her grey eyes knowing I would not be the first to look away.

The bee noises sounded at one moment far off and the next moment inside my head and the garden was so bright my eyes seemed shut and this was a picture of a garden burned on my eyelids. My grandmother was a black shadow standing like a paper doll against the bright garden and I was a paper doll too, swaying backward and forward. I kept my lips pressed tight and made spit back of my teeth with the tip of my tongue. If she moved toward me, I'd spit on her. But she did not move and I could not.

After a while she was no longer black nor the garden so bright nor the bees so close in my head. But we didn't move. What if we were to die here like this? What if we never moved? The grass would grow tall around our legs. Then it would snow and the snow would pile up and maybe bury us.

Her face was twitching now. A muscle in her cheek was jumping. I wanted to laugh. But I thought about how much I hated her. "You won't break my spirit." I had heard the words somewhere and about my grandmother. "You won't break my spirit, you won't break my spirit you won't. . . ." I said over and over till the words ran together in the glare and hot silence like pats of butter and I could both see and hear them but they had no meaning because she was staring and her eyes ran together like the pats of butter and the words and there were her eyes in the pool of butter and my marbles in the sand pool and the words and bee noises in my head. The garden was bright, then dark. After a long time the garden turned bright again and there was a sob in my throat. I could not swallow now. My right knee was trembling and I felt like I was going to sit down without wanting to. She did not move.

I couldn't cry now or sit down or run away. I didn't know what to do. I dried my palms against my wet shorts and remembered to press my lips together again, tight, to show her how much I hated her though now I didn't hate her as much. Now I could imagine leading her down to show her the marbles in the sand pool and pressing up close to her and smelling the dusty lemon odor of her starched dress. I said it over and over: "I hate you I hate you. . . ." But the words lost their meaning and left me with nothing to keep my face mean and my lips tight and my backbone stiff. "It's a silly game we're playing," I said to myself, "and I can quit any time I want to." I could feel a smile in my eyes and I wondered would she know it was a silly game and that we could quit. I could feel the smile on my lips.

She lifted her chin and the line from the corner of her nose to the corner of her mouth deepened. It was not a smile and not a sneer, but a proud look as though she'd won. "It's a good thing you changed your mind," she said. She lifted her head higher and picked her way through the border and up the walk.

I hadn't lost. I hadn't looked away. I was still standing

there in the same spot. She hadn't won, she hadn't! I wanted
to pick up a rock and throw it at her. I wanted to run across
the stream and sit in the dugout. My knees were trembling
and I sat down in the grass and tried to think about nothing, not even about the ant that was crawling up a blade of
grass and waving its feelers against the air. I bent my head
low and asked it my question: "Which'd you rather be run
over by: a new Greyhound bus or an old one?"

IN LATE August the dime store windows were full of note-
books and yellow pencils. In three weeks school would be
starting and I was homesick. Uncle Nat was acting funny
and hardly spoke to me at all. He wouldn't come into the
garden if I was playing in the creek and he wouldn't come
upstairs if I was in the house. He had, though, one day
when I was in the dugout, come up to his room and taken
the toy airplane. I didn't care but I wouldn't even look
through his window to see if he had it hanging up in his
apartment.

My grandfather would walk me down to Five Points and
explain that it was not my fault but to stay out of Grandmother's way because she was worried and sleepless about
Nat. The only thing I heard her say about it though was: "I
wish we could afford Will Jason one day a week. He could
get Nat interested in gardening or in something, I believe."

But Grandpa said he didn't think Mr. Robins would let Will come and add the cost to the unpaid drug bill. "I don't know how much longer he'll let me have pipe tobacco."

Twice I wrote to my mother to come and get me, but I didn't tell her that my grandmother and Uncle Nat would hardly speak to me. She had written back that the last peaches had been shipped and that next week she would go into town and have the furniture moved and would send for me.

I wrote and told her please to send now. I wouldn't be in the way. Please, I could help her with the furniture if she would send for me. I didn't mention what was happening to Uncle Nat and how my grandparents were worried. The next evening she telephoned long-distance and explained that it would be easier her way, that I'd been a brave boy all summer and couldn't I be brave a week or so longer? She spoke to Grandpa and then to me again.

"Yes," I had to say, even with my grandparents listening. "Yes. I know you love me."

Then, because she kept asking, I had to say with them listening: "I love you too." But then I couldn't say "goodbye" when she said "goodbye." She waited for me to say something or to hang up and finally she said, "Hang up, darling." I could hear my breath in the phone and could smell the dusty telephone smell, but I couldn't say anything.

"Hang up, darling," she said. "So I can hang up too." I

knew she meant it was costing money but I couldn't say "Goodbye." I put the receiver back on the hook and went upstairs without speaking to my grandparents who were watching me and lay down on the rug in the middle of the room and studied the string dangling from the fan.

THE REST of the week I stayed away from the house as much as possible. In the mornings I worked on the dugout; but when I started back to the house for a plank, I could see Uncle Nat standing in the garden, not with a hoe or mallet, but just standing. Then when I would come out on the creek bank he would be gone.

The next week there was a cool breeze across the garden every morning. The sky was September blue and clear all day without a cloud. One noon when I was hopping across the stream, late for lunch, I heard shouting near the house. I stepped back and waited, not hiding, but not in plain view. Uncle Nat was walking back and forth shouting up at the house: "I'll be damned if they do!"

He ran into his apartment and slammed the door. No one was in the yard, but then I saw my grandmother's head in the kitchen window. I turned and started back to the dugout, but thinking that she had perhaps seen me, turned again, and jumped from stone to stone across the creek.

Lunch was not ready. The green beans had burned to the

bottom of the pot. The kitchen was full of smoke. In the dining room the iced tea was poured and the ice already melted. In the kitchen my grandparents were both talking at once in sudden spurts, then they were quiet, then talking again, one, then the other, then both, too excited to finish anything.

Sitting in the dining room behind the swinging door, I finally understood: my father had lost his job a month ago. My mother had discovered it when she went for the furniture. He could not afford an apartment for her or for himself. My grandparents had no money to send her. The money from her summer job would feed us for awhile, but would not be enough for rent. She was giving my father fifty dollars so that he could go to California where he claimed he could get a job. She would have to come here to live.

Grandpa began in a loud voice: "Then she'll have to take an upstairs room. . . ."

"I will not have her telling me. . . ."

"All right, then." Grandpa's voice dropped and was calm. "What else can we do?"

"Nathan's got to listen to reason." Grandmother's voice was full of anger and tears.

"And what *is* reason?" he asked in an even, calm voice as though he were talking to a baby.

"He'll have to move back upstairs and let them have the basement."

"That's what you wanted all along." His voice was angry again. "Isn't it?" I could hear him push back a chair and walk to the window.

"Don't say that's what I want!" Grandmother said. Suddenly her voice dropped and she said quietly, "I'm trying to do what's best for everybody."

"Poor Nat," Grandpa said. "It's all he has. . . ."

"Besides"—my grandmother's anger was back—"two women cannot live in the same house together. This way she'll have hers, I'll have mine."

Again there was shouting in the yard. Uncle Nat was under the kitchen window. "I knew it! I knew when I was painting this goddamn basement that Fred would get it."

"Fred's going to California for God's sake!" Grandpa hollered out the window.

"That's right," my grandmother said. "Tell the neighbors."

"They're not going to have it. I'll burn it first." The basement door slammed shut.

"If she'll sell most of that awful, new-looking furniture," my grandmother was saying, but I didn't listen to the rest. I drank a glass of warm tea and took two corn muffins which had already been split and buttered and went out the front door and through the side yard to the creek and across it to the dugout.

LATE THAT afternoon when I came back up through the garden, I could see Uncle Nat standing in the exact middle of the big window. The curtains were drawn on either side of him and he stood without moving. I tried not to look at him, but I kept glancing up. If I told him it wasn't my fault, that I didn't want his old basement . . . if I told him we'd move out as soon as my father got a job . . . but that wouldn't fool him . . . it didn't even fool me. Shoot! He couldn't even hold a job here.

But I was trying to think of words to say in case he stepped out and blocked the path. He was staring, though, at something way above my head, off in the woods. I wanted to turn to see what he was seeing, but I kept on walking up the path and around the house without stopping.

As I went to sleep that night a wind was scraping oak leaves against the window screen and across the slate roof. Once in the night I was half awake and heard voices in the hall. Grandmother and Uncle Nat were talking and she was saying: "I'm glad you changed your mind."

During breakfast the next morning my grandparents did not speak. In the silence I planned what I would say to Uncle Nat if I had a chance. I wouldn't mention his apartment, my father, or anything about where we were going to live. I'd simply tell him about the new steps to the dugout. If he wanted to go and look at them, he could go with me.

As soon as my grandmother folded her napkin, I asked to be excused and ran down, hoping to find him in the garden. He was still standing between the curtains, staring over my head at the same spot in the woods. He did not move. Had he been standing there all night? Had I dreamed the wind and the voices in the hall?

"Uncle Nat," I said, not loud. He did not hear. "Uncle Nat," I said with more breath, then softer. "You want to see the dugout?"

Still he did not move. I stood close to the window. His eyes were open but he was not blinking them. I tapped on the window to make him blink, to make him look at me. "Uncle Nat!" I called.

He did not blink. He was still staring. I rapped louder. "Uncle Nat!" I could not see him breathing either. "He's dead!" I thought. I moved back from the window and screamed: "Grandpa!"

Both my grandparents came to the kitchen window, but I could not look up or away from Uncle Nat standing between the curtains staring out at that spot in the woods, not blinking, not breathing.

"What is it?" they were both asking but I couldn't tell them or look away. With my grandparents coming down the steps I was no longer afraid. I knew he was not dead. "Uncle Nat," I tapped on the glass. "Uncle Nat."

Then, behind me, my grandfather said: "Oh, my God."

My grandmother pushed me aside. "Nat," she called. She cupped her hands on each side of her face and peered into the window, a foot away from his face. "Nathan," she said firmly. She stepped back, but he was still staring at the spot in the woods.

"Well," Grandpa said. He was looking at my grandmother as though they both knew something. "This is it."

My grandmother's face had no expression, nor did her voice when she turned back and rapped on the window. "Nat, answer me."

"We'll have to get in," Grandpa said. They were almost whispering but they did not sound afraid, or sad, or anything. They could have been talking about potatoes. "Have you got a key?"

"You'll have to use the skeleton key. It's under the scarf on my dresser." As my grandmother spoke she did not look away from the window, but she said louder, as though she could see Grandpa rounding the path by the corner of the house: "You'll have to go in from the upstairs door." She turned to me. "Run down to Five Points. Tell Mr. Robins to send Will Jason."

"What if. . . ." I began.

"Tell him I said to," Grandmother said, firmly, but quietly.

"What if he wants to know why?"

"Tell him Nathan's sick," she said. "Don't tell anybody else."

As I passed Grandpa he said: "Run, boy. Run." And I said the words to myself all the way to the drug store.

THE NEXT evening everything was settled. A doctor was in the hall making one last phone call. My grandparents were on the side porch trying to close the bent top of a Thermos full of hot coffee. Will Jason was carrying a basket of food to the black U-Drive-It car parked in the driveway. Grandpa and Will Jason would drive all night and be at the state hospital by eight o'clock the next morning. Uncle Nat sat in the front seat staring straight ahead at the street. I stood back of the car, watching.

I wanted to tell Uncle Nat that we didn't want his apartment. I wanted to tell him something to make him laugh. If he would smile, even a little, he could, I knew, quit staring and begin moving again. If they let me stare back at him, I could get him to smile. Or if I could think of something to tell him. But he knew all my jokes and riddles. He knew about the Greyhound bus. I even thought of poems and rhymes I knew and movies I had seen and about the new steps to the dugout.

I moved around the side of the car away from the house and stood near the front window where he sat staring. I didn't try to stand on the running board because he might think I wanted to touch him again. I moved on up to the front of the car, still trying to think of something to say. He didn't seem to notice me. I eased up on the bumper and onto the front fender and lay down across the hood so that he would have to turn his head if he didn't want to be staring at me through the windshield. The street light was reflecting from the windshield but on the other side I could see his eyes still looking straight ahead. Then I said the rhyme I knew:

> Say, little boy!
> Where'd you get your britches?
> Your mama cut the pattern out,
> Your papa sewed the stitches!

Uncle Nat didn't move. But Will Jason came **up to** my side and said: "What're you doing up there?"

"I'm telling him a rhyme I know."

Will Jason began lifting me off the hood. "I don't think he'll appreciate it," he said. He set me on the ground. Then he watched my grandfather on the porch shaking hands with the doctor. Will Jason walked around to the driver's side and opened the door. He leaned into the car and said:

"We'll be on our way in a minute, Mr. Nat."

Another Love Story

THAT SPRING when he was neither married nor not-married Caleb Jonathon picked up a copy of the *Times* at the red clay airport where the hospital helicopter landed and scanned it as he was being driven to his new office in the Renal Research Lab. At first he didn't realize it was Claire Hamilton's book that had the lead review and it gave him an odd, really odd feeling, like suddenly seeing himself in a hubcap or recognizing that the bones in an X-ray were his own.

"... readers of her richly textured short stories will know how painfully and tenderly her aging and sophisticated protagonist can recall totally and protect zealously those early values: loyalty, heart-breaking grace, and immense style in the face of emotional distress and above all. . . ."

Surely she would not have put him in the novel. Though the two women had never met, she was the only woman Hazel, his wife, had ever been jealous of and it could be all that was needed to end the marriage which for a year had been all front anyway—cocktail parties together and bedrooms in separate wings of the house.

That week he read the book in his office, hiding it between readings in his desk drawer. Even in his depression, now chronic, he was both relieved and disappointed that Claire seemingly had not remembered the summer at all.

He wrote her, as he did from time to time (mainly about the book), but mentioning his depression which disappeared for three or four months at a time and just when he thought he was permanently over it, returning worse than before. ("I know how zoo animals feel," he wrote, "when they dream of the veldt and wake to hear the keeper clanging the gates shut.") She had written back immediately, an impeccably friendly note but had added at the bottom of the page: "I could barely stand to read your sentence about the zoo animals, the veldt." And that was that. Or at least he thought so.

The following winter, though, "Local Talk," a box in the small university-town newspaper, noted that Claire Hamilton had a story in a current magazine "concerning a depressed woman, sick of her husband, her mean and crazy lover, and afraid of an avaricious landlady, who returns from San Francisco to seek solace in the small Southern town where she had been a wildly attractive girl." The item continued that she was the daughter of Dr. Victor Hamilton and the late Agnes Hamilton whose eighteenth century house, Fairmont Bluffs, had recently been bought by the Preservation Society. He breathed again when he saw that it did not say that the man in the story was Dr. Caleb

Jonathon who lived with his lovely wife, Hazel, on St. Martin's Road.

After he had read the story, "Enough to Scare the Loons," about how she had laughed all summer, he realized it had probably been the sale of the old house where she was born that had prompted the story and not (he was sure in his depressed state) any urgent memory of him or any message to him. In fact he had been described in shades of red and straw, the colors of the Piedmont South and was really part of the Southern landscape that had been, that summer, curative to the homesick woman. He had liked the story except for one thing: Gertrude Stein always said she didn't like it when the author said the characters sat down to a good meal and didn't say what they ate. In the same way, Claire had said they laughed but really didn't say what about. It had been almost ten years but he knew exactly what they had laughed about and how and why and not just the sort of family jokes about his car, but also about Roscoe and the Troll, and the grasshoppers and the sensational hiccoughs.

In the story she'd turned him into a psychiatrist, which was flattering and probably necessary. Who, after all, could be romantic about a urologist? Though his work was the first thing they'd laughed about. Sitting by the pool, where the cocktail party had wandered, she'd said, concerning her father whom she adored and hated: "Where did you and Vic meet?" She recrossed her splendid long legs, the voile summer frock clinging to them, as later he learned she always did when mentioning her father.

"Over a glass of pee," he said.

"Tea?" she asked.

"Pee," he said.

She looked into her silver julep mug. "Isn't it true?" she asked. "Southerners always think they can serve rotten bourbon if they give it to you in a silver cup." She took a sip. "But I wouldn't call it tea." She crossed her legs again. "Where did you meet?"

"In my lab." He explained he was in kidney research.

"Then you did say 'pee,' didn't you?"

"Yes," he said, "his."

She'd started laughing in a way that shook her entire body. As if she'd never laughed before. The whole party, to which Vic had invited everyone in town over sixty years old to meet his daughter, had been summer-outdoor-formal: that is to say everyone was assuming casual stances and poses under the huge oaks, and under the lanterns, in and near the hammocks, and on the arms of the wooden lawn chairs, and now near the pool, but still the talk was as mundane as if they were pushing grocery carts.

She was laughing as if she couldn't stop, a startling sight, as if a statue had suddenly laughed and gone on laughing, refusing to be a statue again. Until that moment she'd looked frighteningly sophisticated, the sort of woman he couldn't deal with, her blonde hair parted in the middle and pulled back in a loose bun at the nape of her neck. A beautifully rounded forehead, the kind of high forehead less beautiful women hide under bangs, heavy eyelids, and the most sensual, half-open mouth in the world. But then she'd laughed and all her Radcliffe, Rome, and San Francisco poise had gone and she looked ten years younger and, for the first time, he allowed himself to stare at her magnificent legs. Her flanks under the voile could have been those of a professional tennis player; and her divided calf muscles, which looked hard when he first saw her standing by the bar, now hung soft from the outstretched shin. (Did he remember that she had been a diving champion at Ashton Hall and at college?)

When he looked up, her eyes were soft, her mouth parted in that sensual way. How long had she been watching him, how long not laughing? She asked: "What are you thinking?"

He told her the truth. "That I'd bet on you."

"To do what."

"To win."

She'd fallen silent then and her look was too serious, too experienced. She wet her lip with her tongue and leaned back, always staring. He wanted to say "I can't," without knowing what it was he couldn't do. If she'd laugh again he wouldn't be afraid of her.

"What?" she was asking, leaning toward him again, demanding at least his thoughts. Close. Too close. Too intimate. Her breathing. It was as if the sun had suddenly set. Or a pool light gone out. The dark was closing in on them, the music far away. The air too hot. Her perfume or breath or the fragrance of some shrub (Vic's gardenias) too heavy.

"I didn't want to meet you," he said.

She wrapped one long foot, now out of its slipper, around the bare ankle of her other leg. "What had Vic told you about me?"

"That you were brilliant."

"And that's what you expected."

He nodded.

"Well I am!" she said in a sudden tough New York accent. It was for some reason funny and that was when he knew he'd be seeing her all summer. He had come here to this small Southern town to work, to allow his wife (who had to live within sight of her mother) to claim desertion, to cure himself of ever being romantic again. After all, he was, as his wife reminded him, almost forty.

"Darling," Claire was saying, "don't look so serious." His wife had never once in their entire fourteen years ever called him "darling." Yet it had never sounded more natural, more right for him. Under her heavy gaze he felt darling.

As if to say "Let's be honest with each other," she said, "I'm here trying to straighten out my life. I know I won't stay here and I'll probably go back to San Francisco because Simon (who's here with me) is ten and loves his school. But I don't know whether I'll go back to my husband." She gazed at him. "I rather think not. I mean I really can't bring myself to think about it. And you?"

"More or less the same." He knew it was not idle talk; that actually they were making, as honestly as possible, their commitments to each other for the summer. "My wife and two daughters are in Boston. We're legally separated." He didn't tell her the important part: the separation was going to leave him financially strapped. He'd accepted a low salary here in order to work with Grockens and his famous breed of mice. He had rented a house he couldn't afford and had finally, for that and other reasons, been forced to take two rooms in an old colleague's house. In short, he was living like a first-year resident again, without a penny to spare.

People were coming up to say goodbye and Agnes, her mother, had sent word by Simon that she should be near the front porch so people could find her and she'd begged him not to leave but he wanted to be by himself, to think, not simply to act on impulse.

Her mother and Vic were already standing at the front steps and reminded her of Southern ways: "When they see us talking to each other they'll know it's time to leave." And then Agnes had added: "Except for Louise Kroll, who'll never learn." She indicated a short, dumpy mushroom of a woman, the only one with hat and gloves. "And of course we hope you will stay, Caleb."

"Yes!" Claire took his arm. "Who is she? That voice!" Louise Kroll's penetrating Midwestern voice from way across the lawn was explaining Fairmont to three people: ". . . the deep eighteenth-century fenestration. But the porch is much later. Mid-Victorian."

"Listen to her, giving a history of the house and it's the second time she's been here." Vic relit his pipe.

"Why is she here at all?" Claire asked.

"Because she says such astounding things to people and about people and she never seems to know whose cousin she may be talking to or about. We are bored with the same old people you know."

"She's so busy climbing," Vic said, "she doesn't know which way is up."

"I would assume," Agnes was assuming as she did when she was quite drunk and more indiscreet than she would allow herself to be sober, "that any direction would be."

Claire had walked him to his old car which he'd parked

on the river road below the Bluff. He'd parked there, he explained to her, so as not to embarrass her father. "He's such a snob," she'd said, neither ashamed nor proud of the fact, but as if she were talking about some childish habit of her son. On the way to the car (they were at the boxwood entrance) Louise Kroll had headed them off. "Here comes the Troll," he'd warned her too late. Louise Kroll introduced herself and came on too hard with invitations and flattery and barely acknowledging Caleb's presence. Claire had asked going down the drive "Why does she hate you so" and he, astounded by her perceptiveness, had only said "Yes, I suppose she does hate me." Maybe he would tell her later.

"But I will see you soon," Claire had said, taking his hand. "Tomorrow maybe."

He was in the old car by then and when he said yes definitely he would come back tomorrow, she had leaned in and pressed her hand to his cheek. And then the damned car wouldn't start. Up until then their timing had been perfect, understood, and she, even then, had the grace to laugh just enough before waving and saying she really had to get back before her mother fell flat on her face. There was nothing to do but sit there and wait. He watched her in the rearview mirror and in his alcoholic musings thought it was a delightful name for such a mirror.

So it had begun, their summer of partying and laughing

and making love and forgetting about their immediate pasts, and talking about absolutely nothing serious on their long night walks and swims. He could not at the moment remember when they'd first made love except that it had happened in the cool after a thunderstorm, outdoors (there was no privacy in the small town that summer, no place they could go), at the pool, or the river beach, or in the boxwood arcade. And it had seemed entirely natural and inevitable. He could remember after the first time: he'd dozed off and waked when she began touching his face with her fingertips. It was quite chilly and he had made her lie back, near the water, and had scanned her body with his fingertips and eyes. As certain as he was of the distant crowing of a rooster that he would find the evidence of violence on her. Finally, unsure now, he started to kiss her again, thumb under the angle of her left jaw, and there it was, the scar tissue he had known he would find. He'd turned her head on the grass and kissed the scar and asked: "You won't try that again, will you?"

"Is that what you were looking for?" she whispered and when he nodded she asked how he'd known.

"When you've washed the poison out of as much blood as I have," he said, "you get a feeling about people." She'd never realized that it was the residents in urology who sat through thousands of hours monitoring the machines hooked to those people who had tried to end it with drugs or poison. Neither he nor Claire ever mentioned it again and in many ways his finger palpitating the soft gristle under her jaw had been the seduction scene, the skillful, penetrating, uniting moment; and for weeks afterward, he felt that that intimate knowledge was what they were covering up with their laughter, which excluded almost everyone.

The only person that summer who wasn't excluded by it was Roscoe Thornton, the black athlete and singer who came to the campus one evening for a concert and whom Claire had once given a "marvelous" party for in San Francisco. They'd met Roscoe at the airport with the idea of taking him to dinner and then on to the concert, or if he preferred, which Claire remembered he would, to the concert and then to dinner. When they met him he had an envelope in hand and said in the deepest, most beautifully modulated voice in the world that he'd agreed to go to a Mrs. Kroll's.

"Oh, no, Roscoe, you can't," Claire said. "You mustn't." On the way into town they'd told Madam La Troll (as they now called her) stories: the puce luncheon she'd given for Claire, with puce lettuce and puce placemats and fingernail polish and lime jello and seedless puce grapes in sour cream, and a puce bowl of nasturtium leaves in the center of it all. ("I think maybe she was trying to tell me something," Claire had said.) And the French-American dinner she'd given for a couple from the French Embassy: hamburger with Bearnaise sauce, apple pie and a Lafitte Rothschild champagne. And the beer and pretzel cocktail party for the new head of the German department. "No, Roscoe, she's . . . you just can't go there."

Roscoe was fascinated (and gentlemanly enough to insist on going through with the invitation he'd accepted). "You think she'll give me black-eyed peas and hog jowl?"

Claire had said, "Darling, if I thought it would be that good I'd go."

Caleb could hear only the 'darling' and stood there while they talked about friends they'd known in Rome and then Roscoe had checked the invitation and read: "Please bring anyone, your whole entourage if you like." Together, in spite of his jealousy, he and Roscoe convinced her she was an entire entourage and must go.

For two hours Caleb sat in his lab with growing, pan-icky jealousy, seeing nothing in his microscope, glancing impatiently at his watch. (Had she or hadn't she called him "darling" and why had she not mentioned that they had known each other in Rome?) At midnight when they had promised they'd be standing in front of La Troll's house, he drove up.

They came out silently and didn't begin talking until they were in the car. "Hurry, let's go," Claire said. And then she and Roscoe began laughing. Caleb understood then why all summer everyone, especially Vic, had considered their laughter rude. It was excluding.

"She served. . . ." Claire couldn't say for laughing what she served.

"Oh, man!" Roscoe said in his beautiful accent. "Oh man . . . drive on."

"She served. . . ."

"Hominy grits?" Caleb guessed. "Cornbread? Chitlins?"

"Worse. . . ." Claire gasped. She'd never laughed that hard with him.

"Oh . . . oh . . . oh." Roscoe sounded in pain.

"She served. . . ." Claire finally exploded. "Watermelon."

They told it all over again at Claire's where they stopped for a drink before Roscoe's plane. Vic and Agnes were quite drunk and quite charming and Vic told a townful of La Troll stories. "She kept telling people," Agnes said, "that she was going to give a party for the Fairmont Bluffs when we got back from Europe. Apparently she'd seen the name down at the mailbox and assumed it was ours and no one would tell her we were the Hamiltons. . . ."

"Why is she invited places?" It was a rhetorical question in the town.

"She's as tacky as. . . ."

"Catsup," Roscoe said.

"Precisely," Claire added as if she'd known what he was going to say.

"Where does all the bread come from?"

Vic, when he understood the question, explained about the dead husband who had been a big name in Chicago pork. She'd done the money scene and now she was doing the intellectual, Agnes assumed.

While they talked, Caleb moved to the steps where Claire was sitting alone. Without turning she said: "Why does that woman hate you so much? Were you ever lovers? Did you ever make love to her?"

"Never," he answered. He wouldn't tell her that what had saved him in the face of her persistence was the simple fact that her elastic girdle gave off the same slightly ammoniac smell as the wet newspapers in the mice nests. (He'd come home one Saturday to find the girdle on his desk and her upstairs in his bed and had walked out furious.) He couldn't tell anyone he had tried to spare the woman such a confrontation. Even when she had hinted at near blackmail in her pursuit of him. ("Is something wrong with you? Several people have started asking me.") And later when, too broke to pay the rent, he had sublet half the house to an Iranian man, an old colleague had taken him aside and said: "Why don't you find some other way of cutting expenses, even taking a smaller place?" When pressed for a reason, the old doctor had said: "Women like Louise Kroll can be silly and damaging. Talk. In the long run it makes no difference. But until you get tenure. . . ." And so he had taken the two confining rooms in the very quiet, respectable house.

As they rode back from the airport in brilliant moonlight, Claire continued to admire Roscoe's tremendous poise in face of La Troll's (intentional? one wondered now) gaucheries. Apparently she'd tried to find out if Roscoe was there to see Claire or Caleb and where he would be spending the night. "Then she started making stupid innuendos about your sex life and I simply said: 'Louise, Roscoe is going to Atlanta tonight to see his parents and I am spending the night with Caleb.'" (Everyone had been silent and no one had known whether to believe her; but after that none of his old friends came to him again to say he should try to keep Louise Kroll from talking so much.)

"There's not much of the night left," Claire had said that night, or another one, later, as they walked down the dusty river road. In the distant pines cicadas were singing a dry autumn song, the corn in the little garden was burned to the stalk, and grasshoppers flew up out of the tall straw weeds along the ditches. There was a fall chill in the September air and the moon seemed quite near, as bright and cold as a winter moon.

She would be going soon and yet they'd never talked. He'd

gathered from her remarks to Simon that they would not be living with his father when they returned to San Francisco. And one night her crazy lover had called and she had told him firmly, yes it was better he leave the Bay Area. In any case not to count on seeing her again. But he did not know until he read her story that the courage for such moves came from having returned home where she discovered largely through him that she was as attractive as she'd been as a girl, to have become, in fact, for him a girl again with her flouncing dresses and famous white shorts and flattering laugh. (To be, in short, as the review had said, a woman "whose fictional world encompasses with equal authority the innocence of remembered childhood and the joy and acceptance of adult passions, both tempered with a considerable and mature intelligence.")

"Darling," she said as they reached the grass beach, turning him toward her, "there's something I want to ask you. . . ."

Now would come the outpouring. All the things unsaid that would demand answers and unsatisfactory explanations from him. Did he love her as much as she loved him? Couldn't he come to San Francisco with her? Later? Could she go and come back? Why did it have to be just this summer and no more? Did he then truly love her? How could he bear to say goodbye?

"What?" he asked.

"Did you know. . . ." she started to confess but then her voice brightened, "there's a grasshopper on your ear?" It was not what she'd meant to say, but once said it took the place of all seriousness. He had seen her realize that that was all she would say. It was the "heart-breaking grace" the reviewer had praised. "Do you mind," she asked, reaching toward the grasshopper, "if I take it off?" And then they laughed until they were lying down laughing.

She had spared him from having to explain how completely broke he was, how in July his wife had chosen, as was her right in the separation agreement, two of the most expensive prep schools for their daughters. How now he would have to choose always the cheaper label, hope that his khakis, sneakers, and suede-patched jackets would seem like an affectation and be accepted as such, buy no-iron shirts instead of good cotton batiste. He knew if he admitted even any one of these troubles they would try to figure a way for him to follow her to San Francisco and there was no way. He had looked at her and known it was all right, that whatever was going to happen to her in this life the worst was over. They were staring at each other knowing they were going to leave everything unsaid.

The whites of her eyes were as always, like a child's, without a trace of yellow or of tiny red skeins. Blue-white.

"What are you thinking when you look at me that way?" she asked.

"What a fine set of kidneys you must have. And liver."

For once she did not laugh at an attempted joke. (In her story she said the woman had cried and made a scene but she was only dramatizing her feelings, not reporting what happened.) She had merely turned away from him and when she looked back her face was troubled. They lay for a long while hearing the cicadas and not the slow river and finally she touched his cheek with her fingertip. "Darling," she whispered, "your face breaks my heart."

"Mine, too," he said, meaning hers killed him too when it was so troubled, but it was the funniest thing anyone had ever said and they both knew the moment which could have ruined it all had passed and before they quit laughing they were already naked and making love and then was when he got the hiccoughs. Quietly they tried to ignore it, but they could feel laughter trembling in each other's bodies and she asked in her formal voice: "Nerves?"

"Grasshoppers," he answered and it was glorious, the hiccoughs, the laughter, the rhythm of true love. And at last the final sad stillness of farewell.

The winter after her story came out he was sure he was going to be delivering the summary paper on work with the Grockens mice at the meeting in San Francisco. He told Hazel (whom he had remarried after her mother died) in their new honesty: "I'd like to see Claire while I'm there."

"Alone?"

"You see Dawkins alone." Dawkins was her therapist who led the marathon sessions at the beach. At first she said that was different, but then he'd said, "Alone" and reminded her that she would have to deal with her own jealousy just as he dealt with his when she talked about all the hugging and affection in the T.A. group.

Claire's son had driven her to Ghirardelli Square, an obviously intelligent young man, surprisingly like Vic. Claire was wearing, he was sorry to see, high boots over her marvelous legs, and a tweed suit. She had gained exactly two pounds, both on her hips. She'd let her hair go dark and in places grey and it was cut quite short. She looked exactly what she was supposed to look like: an intelligent, successful author. Her voice was deeper than he'd remembered it and less Southern. She clearly belonged in San Francisco and clearly was enjoying her forties more than she had her troubled thirties. Too, she was enjoying her success (people, other diners, were making a point of speaking to her as they entered). She knew exactly where she wanted to sit in the restaurant and the headwaiter rearranged things so she would have the table by the window with the view of both Alcatraz and the bridge.

For awhile they seemed like strangers sitting over their melons talking about her divorce and second marriage and

Simon's plans to study in Rome, and then about her mother's funeral (she'd been out of the country) and about Vic's new condominium built on the river bank, and about the Preservation Society buying her homeplace and having to sell off the swimming pool and tennis courts to raise money to replant the boxwoods and tear off the Victorian porch.

Claire said: "I was afraid that awful woman would buy it."

"Louise Kroll?"

"But that's not what we called her."

"Madam La Troll."

"Whatever happened to her?"

"She finally got to be mayor and then she just sort of dropped out of sight."

"She didn't have far to go." Claire laughed and then said, "I hate it when I sound like Vic. I'm really not that mean anymore."

But when he told her he'd heard La Troll was in Arabia they had laughed like always. They were laughing now about the puce luncheon and about his old car never starting and Roscoe and the watermelons, and then everything (even details he told her about Agnes's funeral) was funny and suddenly everything and everyone in the restaurant was funny. A dowager type from Burlingame came and stared at them through and over a horn-rimmed lorgnette and finally had said: "Oh! I thought you were two other people." She seemed annoyed that they were not and that she was at fault.

"So did we," Caleb told her.

"But, darling, we are." Claire was choking a bit on her wine.

It was good to laugh again. He'd forgotten how good. How important.

Later, driving back from the little red clay airport, Hazel had asked: "Did you see Claire Hamilton?"

"Yes."

"Did you make love?"

"No," he told her truthfully; they had had lunch together. But he did not tell her that they had laughed like children in church, had been, thus, over lunch, more unfaithful than she could ever in this world imagine.

All fall he kept seeing himself as a funny man, saying and doing things that would have broken Claire up; and by spring his depression had lifted and he was working hard and playing hard and even enjoying being with his wife who, one evening as they undressed after a party, said: "You're easier to live with now that you don't put such constant demands on me."

"What sort of demands?" He was used to the new spill-your-guts jargon. (The "What do you say after you say Screw You" school.) They talked now. Had confrontations.

"Now that you don't put such a heavy trip on me: demanding me to think you're wonderful."

But that's what Claire's story had been about, hadn't it? That if you can have one happy love affair that ends gracefully, then you don't have to keep putting impossible demands on everyone else.

What to Do Till the Postman Comes

THE TWO old men met early each afternoon on the pleasant wide porch and waited for the postman. The porch faced the park, the water, and the afternoon sun. There were glass jalousie windows which could be rolled shut when the winter wind came up across the Tampa Bay.

The two old men, Mr. Beattle, who had been a professor, and Mr. Kelley, a retired manufacturer, were as different in character as one could imagine; and yet this was the time of day they both waited for all morning. It was a time of easy comradeship, free from solitude, and safe from the inquisition of strangers who had no notion of privacy. There was, too, and more importantly, the possibility of mail.

"No, I haven't seen him yet." Mr. Beattle was seated in the light aluminum chair, his walking stick laid precisely across the arms, his feet in their highly polished black shoes and wool-rib socks placed side by side in a spot of sun that warmed the green sisal rug.

Mr. Kelley, breathing heavily, was coming up the three low steps. He pushed open the glass door. "I thought I heard him."

There was no need to comment on this and Mr. Beattle,

who was from Virginia, remained silent in his tidewater way.

It was Mr. Beattle's impressive head that was a surprise each day to Mr. Kelley. Beattle had the sort of thick grey and sandy blond hair that stayed combed but nevertheless stood up and away from his head. With his shaggy eyebrows it gave him a leonine aspect and great dignity. He had practically no cheekbones so that there were slanting hollows from his deep-set eyes to his strong jaw. His teeth, too, in spite of their stains, still showed strong, and added to the vigorous feline countenance.

His body, though, was thin. In winter, when he wore his tweeds, he had the bearing of a large man; but now in the early fall with his sport shirt and narrow knit tie, he was plainly thin and old. Kelley often wondered if Mr. Beattle ate enough.

It was plain to anyone that Kelley had eaten enough all his life. His florid face sagged with weight; and folds of fat hung from his jawbones and swayed when he moved his head. His stomach was enormous and had the padded appearance his grandchildren liked to imitate with sofa cushions. His voice rolled in the deep, hearty manner of many fat men and made Mr. Beattle look smaller, as though he were shrinking to escape the voice which reverberated in the glass sunporch.

"Mr. Beattle," he said, "the sun's still hot."

Mr. Beattle nodded that that was true.

Mr. Kelley let the door close behind him and lowered his weight onto the green web of the aluminum chaise longue. His seersucker shirt was transparent where it stuck to his pink breasts and his green putter-trousers were as wrinkled as pajamas. He wore sandals and no socks. There were days, Beattle was sure, when Mr. Kelley tried to look as repulsive as possible.

On such days, Beattle had further noticed, Mr. Kelley was inclined to make personal remarks.

"Mr. Beattle," he said between breaths, "I don't see how you stand those wool trousers."

With his grey-haired fingers, the yellowed nails pared round and close, Beattle pinched the seams of his worsted flannels at the knees. He was inclined to say that he found them comfortable and was accustomed to them, but that would only open the way for more remarks from Mr. Kelley in his present mood.

When Mr. Beattle said nothing, Kelley watched him shrewdly out of the corner of his eye. He tried again: "Don't you sweat?"

Beattle was certain now that this was a bad day for Mr. Kelley. Even though the question was direct, he chose not to answer.

It was a bad time for Mr. Kelley. For three days he had had no mail. Yesterday he had walked straight from the porch to the Korner Store and had bought things that were not on his list: shrimp creole, poppyseed rolls, French Alsatian wine, a pint of ice cream, four different kinds of candy bars, and promising himself that he would portion these things out to himself over a two-week period, he'd gone home and eaten them all before midnight.

Twice he had awakened during the night with indigestion. This morning he felt not only fat but completely without character and had thought, as Beattle surmised: "To hell with socks. If I'm going to eat like one, I may as well look like one."

When Beattle had waited long enough for the porch to echo with the brashness of the question about his sweat glands, he said, "It is warm today."

Kelley was disgusted with the cautious words. "Why does he have to weigh a damned statement like that? I'm not going to write it down and footnote it."

Beattle was thinking: "Lead him from the personal to the general."

"I sweat," Mr. Kelley said. "I imagine I sweat close to a half-gallon a day."

"That's sixty-four ounces," Mr. Beattle said, not really sure.

"Just about," Mr. Kelley said. "I won't miss it far." He could tell from the tightness about Mr. Beattle's mouth the exact degree to which he was annoying the man. He himself did not like to talk about perspiration and odors; and he respected and admired Mr. Beattle's sense of propriety. Yet, in his present mood, he felt it was good for Mr. Beattle to be offended a little every day. He made a great display now of wiping the creases of his neck and mopping the top of his brown, bald head and even the fringe of his white, curly hair. He stuffed his unironed handkerchief into the side pocket of his putter-pants.

Mr. Beattle, without glancing away from the bay, arranged his black knit tie so that it fell exactly down the center of his checked shirt.

"You haven't seen him yet?" Mr. Kelley remarked again about the postman.

"He'll probably be late today," Mr. Beattle said. "It still being close to the first of the month."

Neither of them spoke or glanced quickly at the other expecting conversation. They were settling now, by mutual, habitual agreement, into that period of silence that lasted sometimes twenty minutes, sometimes an hour, in which they looked out across the green park, at the old people sitting in the sun, or moving slowly with their canes or with their arms clasped to each other for support, along the curving walks, in and out of the sun under the feathery mimosas and the palm fronds which rattled in the constant breeze. Beyond were the yachts in the basin, their tall masts swaying slowly, and the younger men running up and down the wooden docks with buckets and sponges and hoses, calling to each other in the reserved way that people have about boats that are tied up, and calling to and giving orders to the few youngsters who, naked except for shorts and sneakers, jumped from dock to boat deck, shouting in higher voices. And over them and over the bay which lay beyond the boat slips, the seagulls whirled and circled and dived, screeching in their shrill calls which imitated laughter.

From his desk at the double window above the porch, Beattle could view the same scene and even the buoy markers with an indolent pelican on each. But when he was in his apartment he rarely looked down at the boulevard and the park and the sea. In the morning he would glance out at the sky, not to see the clearness of the blue or the shaping of the sea clouds, but to determine what sort of clothes to wear that day. Even during this quiet time with Mr. Kelley, he would watch the people only for a while and then he would read articles and extracts from his academic journals.

Kelley, who had a cottage in the back with a picture window that faced a graveled patio, a sterile banana tree, and a pink stucco wall, surveyed the scene from the porch with immense satisfaction, as though he had arranged it all and was quite pleased with the composition and especially with the line made by the red acacias which bordered the walks.

Sometimes Kelley counted the old people in the park and estimated how much they spent each month and figured in his head how much principal was necessary to yield that monthly income. It pleased him to know that he was surrounded by that many enterprising, conservative, prosperous people, many who, like himself, had started in business in really a very modest way and had been able to hand over to their children quite prospering concerns. His three sons, for instance, the youngest not yet fifty, could all retire tomorrow if necessary.

Sometimes he counted the boats through one window only and figured the capital tied up at that one wooden dock. They represented to him a different sort of wealth and one of which he did not completely approve, even though twice, years ago, he himself had priced boats in showrooms and had escaped only by saying: "Let me phone you back in the morning." The boats would be bought by his sons or grandsons. He himself was too aware of money to spend it so freely. His slight feeling of disapproval was not enough to keep him from enjoying the sight of the full sails as a boat slid out into the bay, tipped, came about, and, gathering the full force of the breeze, skimmed toward the horizon.

Beattle stirred in his chair. The silence, having begun after a rather strained conversation, was not as comfortable as he ordinarily found it, and he wanted to show his equanimity by asking Mr. Kelley a question about the trading on yesterday's market which he was sure to find pleasure in explaining. But judging from Mr. Kelley's hands, curled and relaxed on his stomach, he decided that Mr. Kelley was absorbed in his own thoughts and not troubled by, if indeed he had noticed it, Beattle's early annoyance.

Beattle, too, looked back at the park and played his game. He liked to see it for a few minutes each day as a different painter would see it. He had begun the month before with the obvious choice of Cézanne. He had worked his way through the French Impressionists and then had searched backward through Watteau and the English and now was seeing it as Rembrandt might. He squinted his eyes till only the white sail shone brilliantly against the dark sea, and then opened them wide enough to catch lesser lights from a cloud, a water tank, and the top deck of another boat. He, too, had a feeling of gratification.

Being of a more contemplative mind than Kelley, he realized that the peaceful feeling came, not from the scene itself, but from the usually easy, uncompromising comradeship on the porch. Both of the men respected privacy and both of them had had in their winters here the disquieting experience of making acquaintances too hastily, from fear of loneliness, with people who not only did not revere privacy but who actually did not know that the need existed. As a result, both of them were sensitive to encroachments, their own and others.

Kelley, in one of his first winters here, had generously left his doors open so that his neighbors could come in without being invited, for a drink or to watch his TV which was one of the first sets in the city. One evening he had glanced about his living room—terrace and seen eleven people, three of whom he knew only by name, gazing at, fascinated by, a loud and senseless TV program. He had studied each of the dimly lighted, expressionless faces and asked: "Do I really like that person?" "Do I want to know him better?" Then he had asked the decisive question, feeling he had earned a right to a certain degree of selectivity: "Would I know that person back home?" The answer in nine of the cases was no. At that moment the two to whom he would have said yes, a frail little lady and her husband, an old lawyer from Vermont with snowy hair and brows, moved toward him, touched his hand and whispered, "Don't, don't," when Kelley started to rise. The lawyer had waved toward the TV set: "I don't understand all this." At the beginning of the gravel drive he clasped

Kelley's hand. "Maybe we can talk some evening." But Kelley was never free in the evening to visit. By the end of the winter he hated the evenings and the people who arrived by habit and sat in his living room until almost midnight.

After that winter Kelley moved with discretion into a new neighborhood. But even then, two winters ago he had left an old preacher in his cottage and had returned to find the man standing before an open shirt-drawer. The man had not seemed ashamed at being caught or even aware that he had been. He announced: "You have thirteen white shirts, six colored, and twenty-three sports shirts." Kelley, therefore, respected and even envied the way in which Mr. Beattle, through training and temperament, managed to keep a proper distance.

Beattle, on his part, however, had learned slowly. He had had to break his lease in one house because an old couple there had tried to adopt him. They had insisted that he eat health foods with them, at least one meal a day. He could still taste with displeasure the dessert which was invariably a protein marshmallow: dry cottage cheese rolled in wheat germ.

In turn, he had been too bold and enthusiastic in one of his own friendships. He had discovered in a bookstore a retired surgeon who had gone to school in Switzerland and spoke French with a beautiful accent. Later over a cup of mint tea they had continued the animated appraisals of Victor Hugo and Balzac, exchanged names and addresses, and after that he had gone often to the surgeon's to speak French. It was thoroughly delightful to Mr. Beattle and he did not realize that his companion was not as delighted as he until he was stopped one day on the stairway by the gentleman's landlady and told that the old surgeon was asleep and was not to be disturbed in the afternoons.

After that when they met, less often and by accident, they still had lively discussions, but Mr. Beattle could not enter into them with the same eagerness as before and was always somewhat apologetic toward the surgeon. The doctor was also apologetic: "I must rest a great deal because of this condition. But there's nothing to prevent us from having dinner together, is there?" The invitation and acceptances remained tenuous; and even when he read in the paper a notice of the surgeon's death, he could not believe wholeheartedly in the "condition" and still felt rebuffed.

Somewhat inadvertently the same thing had happened between Beattle and Kelley. In their early days on the porch the year before, they had talked a great deal about general topics and enough about private ones to give each a feeling of security and to satisfy a natural curiosity before *it* could exceed itself.

Beattle, for instance, knew that Mr. Kelley had made a

comfortable fortune manufacturing metal office furniture, that his oldest son and son-in-law were managing the firm, that Mr. Kelley had been warned by his doctors to retire, and to lose a considerable amount of weight which he had been unable to do. Until her death twelve years ago, his wife had watched his diet and weight for him. He had always traveled a great deal, in North America, and always stayed at the best hotels and eaten the best that was offered. His cottage and patio in the back cost four times as much as Mr. Beattle's upstairs efficiency apartment and yet he felt that he was doing himself an injustice by not buying a house on the Inland Waterway, on the other coast, somewhere above Fort Lauderdale.

Kelley knew less about Mr. Beattle. He knew the man had never married, had previously lived with a sister and her family in a small university town where the brother-in-law was connected with the business part of the school, and that Mr. Beattle had never been head of the department and was, he could not hide the fact from Mr. Kelley who understood the necessity of promotions, in retrospect a little bitter. Kelley did not know and could not determine, but would not approach the subject even obliquely, what exactly Mr. Beattle used for money. He had written to his daughter and asked at the reference room of the library and had gathered that the retirement pay for an associate professor would be very small, less for instance than he himself paid in rent for the little cottage.

The incident which determined the limit of their relationship had not occurred on the porch; and neither of the men could have, at the moment, recalled or recognized it. It was almost nothing at all. One day last fall, Mr. Kelley had told Mr. Beattle that later in the afternoon his car, a two-year-old Cadillac, which had been in storage, would be checked thoroughly and brought to him. He had been rather pleased and said, "We won't have to depend on taxis now."

Mr. Beattle said that would be nice indeed, not realizing that he was included in the "we" since he never called cabs.

That evening he had been pressing a pair of trousers when there was a series of knocks on the door. He had only time to hide the iron in the oven and push the ironing board behind the bookcase so that it could not be seen from the entrance-way, when the knocks sounded again and Mr. Kelley's deep voice called: "Mr. Beattle!"

When he opened the door, Mr. Kelley was breathing heavily but managed to say that the car was out on the street, to come, they would go to an uptown bar together. Mr. Beattle was intent on sniffing the air for the smell of scorched wool and stared at Mr. Kelley blankly. Mr. Kelley had repeated the invitation. Mr. Beattle had thought to himself: "Two dollars for a round and then I'll have to buy him a drink and that'll be my groceries for almost two days." He had declined.

Kelley had gone down the steps, holding to the banisters with both hands, thinking of people he could and should have asked. After all, he and Mr. Beattle were merely porch-acquaintances through necessity. "Still, he could have asked me in." He held to the newel post. "At least till I could get my breath." By the time he reached his car he had thought of a couple he knew who would appreciate a ride along the bay shore and had forgotten Mr. Beattle. But it never occurred to him to ask him anywhere again.

Beattle, on his side, did not feel that he could afford any sort of entertainment. Once every three weeks he bought a fifth of bourbon and had one drink a day, not before dinner, but in the middle of the evening when he knew that if he did not talk to someone he might go insane. Usually he would talk, then, to himself, sometimes in French, sometimes in English, rarely in both. About twice a year he would go on to a second and third drink and finish an entire pint or more. On such occasions he would sing French student songs and dance with a chair and finally fall across the bed giggling and sleep with his clothes on. The next day he would smile fondly at the image of himself dancing and sleeping with his clothes on.

"There he is!" Kelley sat upright in the chaise longue. The postman's shrill whistle could be heard intermittently far up the boulevard. He had still to come to the corner, go up and down the one-way side street, before arriving; but the first sound of his whistle was always the cue for the two men on the porch to begin talking again.

On the other porches other people were gathering. An old man in the park stopped, still bent, lifted his head, and listened. When the whistle blew again, he turned about on his cane in a small half-circle and in tiny scraping steps headed back toward the houses, stopping to listen and to rest and to wipe his forehead with a folded handkerchief from his breast pocket. Soon the park was empty. Only one woman in a crocheted hat dozed on a bench in the sun, her dark glasses slipping down on her sharp nose, her cat on a chain, crouching, watching a bird.

"I won't get anything today," Mr. Beattle said. One of them and sometimes both of them felt compelled to make the statement every day. It was a charm that brought them luck. Then they could be surprised or feign an indifference to hide their disappointment.

"I should," Mr. Kelley said. "I haven't had any in four days. Not even a post card."

The whistle was sharper now and more frequent. They tried not to pause when it blew, but in spite of their efforts it punctuated their conversation, which became more and more animated.

"Still I have to wait," Mr. Beattle said. "Even when I know there's nothing."

Neither of them would use the expression which was heard everywhere that old people gathered: on the benches, in the grocery, at the laundry-store, in the post office, the park and at the barbershop: "It gives me something to do."

"I wish he would come early and get it over with," Mr. Kelley said. "I sleep as late as possible." He had never admitted this before; he listened to the whistle near the corner and went on: "If I wake before six, I take another sleeping pill. Generally I can sleep till after ten."

"I wake at seven every morning," Mr. Beattle said. He'd always had nine o'clock classes.

"Seven!" Mr. Kelley said in admiration and pity. "What do you find to do all morning?" He had not meant to ask and his voice dropped on the word "morning" as though he were trying to negate the question.

Mr. Beattle seemed glad to answer. At least he spoke quickly: "Read. I read." He did not want to say that he swept, and dusted, and dusted his books, and once a week cleaned his typewriter, and cooked lunch and brushed his clothes and spot-cleaned them with damp cloths and naphthas and pressed his drip-dry shirts. All these things he felt would be admitting poverty and Mr. Kelley, with his maid who came twice a week, would think them beneath a man's dignity. "And do research," he said, a little pompously.

The word "research" and the tone annoyed Mr. Kelley and again he felt the need to offend Mr. Beattle. "I stay in bed as long as possible. Then I get up." Kelley waited for the postman's whistle which was on the side street now. "And stand naked in front of the mirror. Sometimes I even pull up a chair and sit naked in front of it for fifteen or twenty minutes."

Mr. Beattle rolled his cane along the arms of the chair and glanced uncomfortably at Mr. Kelley.

"It keeps me from getting off my diet," Mr. Kelley said, gratified at having roused Mr. Beattle. "Then I make my shower last as long as I can." The postman blew again, only three houses away. "Breakfast takes me over an hour with the paper and my coffee."

The postman was too near for conversation. Again, by agreement, they sank back into a silence. Mr. Beattle continued to roll his cane up and down the chair arms. Mr. Kelley rebuttoned two buttons on his shirt. The postman blew again and came up their walk and was now on their steps. He called out the mail as he sorted it between his fingers and dropped it into the five boxes under the awning. "Mr. Beattle, Dr. Beattle, Mr. Kelley, Mrs. McGuire, Mr. Johnston, Dr. Beattle, Mr. Thackston . . ."

"Thackston's moved!" Kelley said.

"Right." The postman picked the letter out of the box. "McGuire and Johnston and that's all." He swung his leather bag back over his hip and started down the steps. "That's all?" Mr. Kelley asked.

"What're you complaining about?" the postman called from the walk. "You got one."

Mr. Beattle already standing was trying not to seem hasty.

"Did I get something?" Mr. Kelley asked.

"He called your name," Mr. Beattle said. He opened the door and stood on the top step picking his letters out.

"Would you hand me mine?" Mr. Kelley asked in a voice that still showed doubt.

Beattle handed him an envelope without glancing at it. Beattle sat down before he began studying his own three pieces. One was from a modern language group and he knew it would be asking for money. One was from a former student who was now teaching and with whom he carried on a regular correspondence even though he could not exactly recall the man's face or appearance or work. The third was a postcard from his sister. He would take them all upstairs and read them over a cup of tea.

Mr. Kelley was plundering his envelope, Beattle noticed,

in the way a small boy would open a box of chocolate crackers. Kelley read without glasses, holding the letter some distance away and to one side. He was grinning and once he laughed. "Well, well," he looked up at Beattle as though he were a stranger, "my baby grandson's walking now!"

"That's what babies eventually do, isn't it?" Beattle thought, but immediately censored himself for the envy he was feeling. He said nothing and waited for Mr. Kelley to finish his letter.

"Walking!" Mr. Kelley said again. He saw the look with which Mr. Beattle had repressed his feelings. "It's from my daughter-in-law," Mr. Kelley said. He was amused. "She begins: 'There's no news.'" He crammed the letter into his pocket with the wadded handkerchief.

"How old is he?" Mr. Beattle asked.

"Ten months. Walking. She says he's been walking for two weeks," Mr. Kelley said. "He was just learning to pull up the last time I saw him. Well . . ." he said. He looked across the park at the boats in the sun. "I'll have to send him something."

"Shoes perhaps," Mr. Beattle said.

Mr. Kelley laughed but at the same time he thought: I shouldn't have told him.

"Maybe a little boat," Mr. Kelley said. He thought about it and tried to remember where he had seen a splendid toy boat. He would ask one of the youngsters on the dock. When he thought of the youngsters he remembered their sneakers and that he had seen in the dime store red sneakers for babies, not as long as the width of his hand. "Shoes, that's not a bad idea," he said.

Mr. Beattle felt pleased with himself and no longer envious in the least. He pulled himself up and stood with his cane poised and watched Mr. Kelley seem to spread out in the sun which slanted across the chaise longue.

"Are you going to the grocery?" Mr. Beattle asked. It was, in essence, an invitation since he was standing nearer to the glass door than to the hallway.

"Not today," Mr. Kelley said, folding his hands across his ponderous stomach. "I think I might doze awhile." He watched Mr. Beattle going down the boulevard, swinging his cane in perfect unison with his left leg, and watched the palms swaying in the park, and beyond the park, the masts swaying and the youngsters still jumping from the boats to the docks and back again. He let his eyes close for a moment and could still see the white sails and the seagulls wheeling in the bright sun.

The Death of a Chimp

FOR A week the astronaut had been moping about the house and his wife was beginning to be worried. Since his big and last flight he worked now only in an advisory capacity to the Agency but that was from his own choice. For two years he had seemed quite content and so the recent moodiness seemed not to be directly connected to his retirement. There was nothing to account for it that his wife or those she mentioned it to could see.

She hated to snoop but when she did she found nothing in his pockets in the way of notes, nothing on his desk in the way of unusual bills, and nothing in the car's glove compartment to indicate serious repairs to be made. His medical record was up to date and perfect with an exam not two months past. Yet he definitely had something on his mind he did not want to talk about with anyone.

One morning while she was putting clothes in the dryer, she heard him on his basement shop phone talking. "That's very expensive, isn't it?" he asked. He listened and then he said, "What size animal would that be?" He talked awhile longer, directly into the phone and apparently with his back to her, for he often turned and turned, as if in space, when talking on the phone or sometimes even while watching his wide-screen TV, as if he had learned to comprehend the world better while spinning slowly. In any case she could not make sense of the rest of the conversation. Except she heard him say quite clearly, "No. Say one large as a man."

When he went directly from there to his car she hoped he was not going to buy an animal for her. She had mentioned an Airedale but she certainly did not want to own one: she simply thought their stubbornness was amusing. She went out to the drive and asked as he got into the pickup where he was going. "To drive about," he said. He often did that. She told him lunch would be ready soon, which he of course knew (she sometimes wished he would be a second or two late for anything), but what she wanted to convey was that he did not have time to shop. Especially not for a dog they certainly did not need.

Once he was safely down the street, she went directly to his workshop. There on his desk was the telephone book, opened to the Yellow Pages, with check marks by the names of two taxidermists. Her first impulse was that she did not want an Airedale and certainly not a stuffed one. Though it would be less trouble. As she worked about the house, keeping an eye from time to time on the stove, she thought she might use a stuffed Airedale for a door stop, a towel rack, a bedside dog, a seat by the sink, a watchdog crouched on the front porch or inside the front door, any number of things, but none of which appealed to her enough for her really to wish he might bring one home.

He ate his lunch punctually but without his usual slow and sensuous enjoyment of it. He did not smell the melon, nor the soup; he did not study the color of the roast beef juice nor the French window through the iced tea; he did not drag the ice cream spoon slowly through his lips. He merely ate.

Later walking through the garden, he did not pull up the young radishes to smell the earth on them, nor taste a baby carrot, nor roll the lime-green lettuce leaves against his thumb, nor study as he often did the sky and clouds. True, he turned in a drifting, weightless way, about and about, and scanned the sky and lawn, but he did not seem to be embracing it as he sometimes did, as if he were delighted close up with the amazing blue-and-white-swirling planet he had had God's view of, a view given to him and to few other men.

The astronaut's wife had suspected he might be having an affair which would leave him tired or might be in love which would leave him bewildered. Since his flight, women had found him attractive, not only because he had been for awhile hailed as a hero, but because of the sensual way he tested and tasted the world. It was sexy, the things he did with his tongue and fingertips and eyes, the way he tilted his head toward music. Tired, all that seemed gone from him now.

"What worries you?" asked the astronaut's wife one dawn after they had made love and she had not felt, as she often did, that she was the ultimate end of a splashdown, that she was the first and only woman, his reentry to the world.

"Do I own myself?" he asked.

"Do I seem possessive?" She knew she was. "Overpossessive?" She loosened her arm from about his chest which was turned away from her.

"Oh, not you, darling," he pulled her arm back around him to embrace his chest. "Does the Agency still own me?"

It was a fear he had had before and during his training and sometimes even after he had made his flight. Now it had returned. His voice was again haunted.

They had both been debriefed, had studied his papers and his insurance policies. There were certain countries he could not travel to, certain precautions he must take in travelling, in speaking with men in the media. But there were no oppressive measures or restrictions.

"We are free," the astronaut's wife said.

"I know you are," the astronaut said, "but am I?"

Because she did not know what to say, she said nothing. Silence she had learned in his trainings, in his takeoffs, in his flights and splashdowns. She had been deafened by pure concentration and ultimate love. Now she was silent and did not know she was silent.

"Where will I be buried? Can I be buried where I please? Can I be buried at all?"

The astronaut's wife reminded him he had the right to a military funeral, even burial in Arlington, if he chose, but those were matters for him to decide. It mattered not at all to her where as long as there was a place for her by his side. "I would want that too," he said. And then he said no more before he dropped off as sudden as always into the dark void of sleep, where she was sure that in his dreams he spun slowly slowly through the night sky.

In the months that followed the astronaut did whatever he was asked by his wife and various organizations, but without the enthusiasm he had had following his flight. After Christmas though, he began talking about Washington and maybe going there for a week. In early March they drove over. On the way in they passed the Arlington cemetery and she said, "Should we stop here and look around? It'll be a nice break before the traffic." For in her mind she thought that to find a burial spot was the hidden reason for the trip. He looked about perfunctorily but it was clear he had stopped only because it was her suggestion.

The next morning he stated that he was going to the Aerospace Museum at the Smithsonian to see someone named Ham. He did not ask her and she did not offer to go with him. When they met for lunch under the pyramid he seemed more distant than ever. On the way out of town he interrupted his own long reverie to say: "Body and soul." He had said it often during training, meaning the government owned him body and soul and before his expedition it had been his soul he was concerned about. "Body and soul," he said. "Now it is my body." The astronaut's wife asked what about his body and he said, "I wonder who owns it."

"You do," she said. "Why do you doubt?"

"The government can do anything," the astronaut said with an air of defeat and finality.

For awhile she wondered if he had slipped away during their day in the capital and gone over to Bethesda for some special checkup. When they had been home a week she again went through his medical files but there were no new papers. But of course it was too soon. That night the astronaut's wife did something she had never done before, not even when he was in space.

She went down to his study and locked the door. On his desk, under the Bible, was a walnut humidor which had, in a pouch of tobacco, the key to his big desk drawer. She opened the drawer and searched it for new documents, health reports, insurance policies. But all of the papers seemed to be the ones he had showed her before his final flight.

She locked the drawer, put the key back in the tobacco pouch in the humidor, and was replacing the Bible when she noticed a paper sticking out. It was a copy of a newspaper clipping that said: "Ham, a 26-year-old chimpanzee, the first ape in space, died yesterday at the North Carolina Zoological Gardens in Asheboro, N.C. The ape made his first flight January 31, 1961. Ham has spent almost his entire life with human beings but after the completion of his work with NASA he had been successfully introduced into a colony of apes at the N.C. Zoo where he had bonded with a chimp named Maggie who was with him at the time of his death. His body is being turned over to a taxidermist who will prepare it for permanent exhibition in the Smithsonian Institute."

She was sorry to be reminded that the ape had died. Once they had stopped on a trip to Florida to see Ham in his retirement in the splendid new Asheboro zoo. The wife had expected the astronaut to phone ahead to be allowed to spend time alone with the ape but no. He approached the moat around the chimp's mountain quietly, respectfully, and half-hid among the other visitors. At first he had not seen Ham, but then he had spotted him lying flat on his back in the sun on one of the simulated flat bed rocks. The astronaut had watched, frowned and said, "He's an old man now. Why don't they give him more privacy? He's earned it."

At his desk holding the Bible and the clipping, the wife

remembered finding the phone book open to the page of advertisements for taxidermy and a most unreasonable fear shook her.

The next day they had had lunch at the university with a scientist visiting the Russian department and the planetarium. Everyone at the table had seemed a little puzzled by the astronaut's persistent and really tiresome interest in how the bodies of Lenin and Stalin were preserved well enough to be on display. He had persisted in his questions until he learned the principle was the same as that of the refrigeration in his own home. Cold liquid was circulated through the body and then pumped back into coils where it was chilled again. The visiting scientist had no idea whether the process was patented but he believed it must be since it had not been duplicated outside of Russia.

During the week that followed the astronaut seemed to be recovering from his apathy. He woke early, before dawn, and lay on his back in the grass and watched the stars fade out and the sun come up. He loved again the sound of water as he splashed the shrubbery with the garden hose. He held the breakfast coffee cup to his cheeks and eyelids as though to absorb with every pore the warmth and aroma. He even suggested they go to a large cocktail party from which he could have easily and gracefully excused himself.

At the party she watched him off on his own, gyrating

among several distinguished members of the law faculty which seemed odd but not unusual since wherever he went he asked questions and learned as much as he could. Later she saw him talking to a lawyer who had once been their neighbor, and still later he was on the terrace, alone with an eminent judge.

On the way home he hummed to himself and together the astronaut and his wife sang bits of songs from their college days. When they fell into silence it was a silence as sweet as rain. When he cleared his throat she knew it was not to sing again but to cleanse his soul. "It's against the law in this state and perhaps every state in the Union, for a taxidermist to stuff a human being."

"I'm sure it is," she said.

As he turned the car smoothly into their driveway, he said, as he had always said years ago when life was simple and he was unknown, "Well, jiggety-jig, jiggety-jig, all the way home."

Where She Brushed Her Hair

HERE IN San Francisco the other night we had a party for a friend of ours, a psychiatrist from New York. It was a very bad party: we had invited some psychiatrists and analysts whom we did not know really well, and too many European-born doctors who made the party formal instead of relaxed. They did not drink enough and instead of crowding together in one room, as people do at good parties, they arranged themselves in isolated groups throughout the large rooms which could have held, Kathy whispered to me in passing, three times as many people.

The party was from six to eight and we had expected many of the fifty people to be here until ten or even until midnight. But it wasn't that kind of party. By eight-thirty everyone was gone and Kathy and I were exhausted; a sure sign it was an unsuccessful party.

Suddenly the doorbell rang and Howard and Eve Bryant came back in. They had been the first to leave but they had decided, after looking for a restaurant, that our ham was exactly what they wanted: a ham sandwich each and cold shrimp.

We were pleased for they were the best people to talk over

a party with. Eve and Kathy had been in school together and Howard was easy to talk to and made jokes, the sort of analyst everyone said about: "He doesn't seem like a psychiatrist at all."

The party had troubled him. He'd felt attacked by our New York psychiatrist on several grounds and levels and he wanted to talk. There is nothing that can make a person feel so sane as to comfort a socially wounded psychiatrist; and so after we had eaten ham sandwiches and made fresh coffee, Kathy and Eve went into the living room to gossip and giggle in a schoolgirlish way which neither would ever do with anyone else.

Howie and I moved through the double doorway to my office which tonight had been the bar and there with Irish coffee Howie talked until he'd got all his grievances out and had begun to make jokes about them. It had been an unfortunate gathering of people.

Then, as usual, we began to talk about fiction and fiction writing which seemed to fascinate him more than talk about therapy.

I said: "But why is it that stories have value and people will pay for them and yet everyone is bored by dreams?"

"Bored by dreams!" He could not believe me.

"Maybe not if it's your business," I said, "but I am. I hate to hear dreams. I hate the singsong voice people use to tell them. The monotone. The trancelike stupid look that blanks out all expression in their eyes."

He could not believe I was being serious.

"You can't be serious," he kept saying, which of course was enough to make me exaggerate my boredom. "But you might try, Claude," he said patiently, "just once: writing down your dream and thinking about it and seeing what a story it really is."

We talked on for a long while about authors who had killed themselves and how it could have been predicted, or in some cases could not, from their work, and about Marilyn Monroe and the effect of her death on patients; and then he would come back to dreams and say: "I would suggest you try it. You would, I believe, find it interesting."

I promised him several times I would; and at the gate shook hands with him in promise.

That night I made a special effort to remember my dream when I waked before dawn; and as a result, the next morning was able to record the following:

Dream

The mother is kneeling before her dresser brushing her long black hair steadily, with even strong strokes; caught up in the rhythm of her movements, her thoughts turned inward, her face toward the black silk cloth she has thrown over the rug. She is unaware that anyone is in the room, for indeed, since I am invisible and omniscient, there is not. The door from the dressing room to the bedroom begins to open, and I the dreamer think, no, that is too soon for the door to open; that is only the first two pages of the story; as always you're taking the pace too fast; four more pages should pass before anyone enters, then keep that pace throughout the rest of the story. The door closes and the mother continues, alone, brushing her hair, while I, invisible, watch.

First Thoughts

When I first wake I know that I have stated clearly my most serious problem as a short story writer. Having come at story telling through writing ten-line feature stories for newspapers, I tend to rush through scenes without draining them, without exploring and exploiting the emotions. In addition, and perhaps more important than training is a quirk of temperament; I am afraid of boring readers, losing them by not being instantly likeable, and showing them immediately that there will be action. Only recently have I realized that in my own reading it is not action I like but the musing about the action. The dream, I believe, is trying to teach me something about the pace of a short story, the sexual tension and building and resolution, if you like. But my mind is open—for, perhaps, and most likely, the dream is about something altogether different and has nothing to do with fiction. At any rate, but preferably the slow rate suggested in the dream, to find the true meaning of the dream, let us begin:

The Story

All day she has been anticipating a visitor this evening and the house is ready for the unannounced guest, the food cooked, the table set.

At last it is five o'clock and the mother is alone. She is kneeling on a square of black taffeta which she has used for this purpose all her married life. She was married in 1910 when she was twenty, now it is 1930 and she is forty. Anyone watching her in the dressing room, with the late afternoon sun fractured into rainbows by the stained-glass window of the Victorian house, would think she was trying to gather up the rainbow pieces, or was about to pray, or that a religious rite is about to begin. And in a sense it is, for the things which Ardella Perry learned when she was a little girl—Ardella Phillips then ("Change the name but not the letter/ Change for worse and not for better")—she is faithful to as to a catechism.

Two of these precepts she is keeping faith with now even though each day the faith grows harder to keep. The first and most important is that a lady or gentleman must have at least one hour to himself each day. Her own mother, born in 1845 and married at twenty, the last year of the Confederacy, had always insisted on this hour from five to six each day for herself and for her four daughters. It made no difference what each chose to do during that hour in so far as they were not within sight of each other, not making noise or calling out, and not engaged in activity which was like the endless work they pursued during the rest of the day.

"Leisure time" Mamma had said and "Mamma" was pronounced not at all Southern and slow, but quickly and with a rising lilt the way Ardella's grandmother had admired children saying to their mothers, before the War, in Paris. "Leisure time, you must learn to use it as ladies do: needlework, not darning and mending, mind you, but pretty work—crocheting, tatting, embroidery." There was something Mamma felt was common about knitting, and even though they were as poor as all their upcountry Carolina neighbors, and needed knitted stockings just as badly, during that hour of privacy they never knitted. "Read: the Bible, Shakespeare, *The Almanac*, Scott . . . or better still, think. Reflect. A lady needs to reflect. Look back over the day to see if she has in haste offended anyone, has failed to be kind where kindness was needed. And when isn't it needed? Well, there are people who will abuse kindness and take it for weakness, and it is your duty to teach these people, who lack training, to distinguish." Mamma had now been dead since 1904, and yet Ardella, picking up the bone-handled comb from the towel, can hear every soft word as clearly as if they were still living in the overseer's house on the edge of what had once been Grandpapa Moore's plantation.

Ardella throws her long black hair over her head. It is damp from being wrapped in a towel during her bath, and the breeze from the sleeping-porch window feels cool from her neck all the way to her waist where even the ends have felt heavy in the heat.

The house is quiet for a moment, as if a baby were asleep. The twins are still at the library and music. The two small girls are at peace with their game of Pollyanna on the side porch beneath the sleeping porch. Such moments are rare and in such moments she realizes how fast time and her life are going by. And she, she has so little time to herself she hardly knows any longer who she is. She is the house, the children, her husband, the trucks, the vegetable garden; she is all these things that occupy her waking hours, so that like a dreamer she is all things and nowhere, every person and yet alone. It is only when she comes here to comb and brush her hair, not a hundred strokes, but a thousand, that she persuades her soul back into her body, recoups her strength, apportions her energy to the one most in need of it at the moment, thanks her God for her magnificent body and vitality, her appetite, digestion, and health. This is the gift for which she is most thankful and where does health show to better advantage than in a beautiful head of hair? Where, even the Bible asks, is a woman's glory?

How does Nola, she wonders, stand her head bound up even on the hottest days. She likes much that is old-fashioned about Nola, her beautiful manners, but on these days she should be bareheaded. Her temper would improve, Mrs. Perry feels sure.

This morning she had started to mention it again but had not gotten very far. Sometimes Nola knew what she was going to say and stopped her with a glance. She had begun and got no further than "Nola, it's going to be another hot day."

Nola nodded, unsmiling.

Mrs. Perry had not slept well at all and already she had made coffee and cut the biscuits, still on the dough board, before the cook, still in her hat, let herself in, humming a comforting song, neither jazz nor church, to herself. Nola said simply good morning and nothing more while taking off her hat and pinning on her head cloth. Mrs. Perry was standing, coffee cup in hand, trying to recapture the dream which troubled her sleep and finally waked her. Whatever the dream—it eluded her completely now—she had waked with the sense that someone was coming today.

"Somebody," she says, trying to be cheerful in the face of Nola's sullenness, "is coming. . . ."

"For dinner?" Nola asks, ready to be all day cantankerous if more work is added.

"I don't know. I feel like we should be ready."

Nola says nothing but turns her back as she pours her tin cup of coffee.

Mrs. Perry is quick to avoid trouble: "We'll just have Sunday's dinner tonight. Sunday you can take off."

Nola is partially mollified but considers first the idea, then the taste of the coffee. She approves of neither: "You sure don't know anything about making coffee. You got to use a lot of grounds to make good coffee. That's one thing you can't skimp on." She implies a criticism of the way the house is lately being run. "Depression or no Depression."

Mrs. Perry has suspected the coffee did not taste right. "Make another pot and I'll drink this."

The two women know just how far to push, how far to pamper each other, and establish their working relationship for the day before the husband and children come down to breakfast.

"Company," Nola says, pouring the weak coffee into a saucepan. "But you don't know who."

"I'll invite Deliah and we'll kill a chicken and if no one shows up we'll simply call it Sunday dinner."

"On Friday night?" Nola says. She allows a musical tone of amusement to well up in her throat.

Mrs. Perry considers herself, as everyone else considers her, a sensible woman. Yet she does listen to her feelings, and more often than not to her presentiments because they (as they are apt to with strong-willed women) do come true.

With thick coffee brewing, the biscuits in the gas oven, Nola feels better. They talk about Deliah, Mr. Perry's sister whom they both adore, and then again Nola feels annoyed. "I suppose you're going to want me to stick around here until after dinner."

"Not if it's only Deliah."

Nola sighs. She feels the need to re-establish the fact that this is not her day for work, much less for company-work. Mention of Deliah takes her out of herself for a while, but now she descends again to her depths. She comes to the surface for a moment when the fresh coffee begins to percolate. "I'd leave have one day off next week, 'stead of Sunday," she says.

To Mrs. Perry it is all the same.

In the face of such easy victory Nola feels the need to explain her mood and request. "I think I'll be wanting me a day of rest come Tuesday or Wednesday."

Now it is clear, Nola's impatience and irritability of the

past few days. Mrs. Perry wishes the younger woman would take aspirin or something at such times instead of upsetting the entire household, bossing the children around, burning everything in the oven.

A glimpse of the dream comes to Mrs. Perry: she herself was standing at the sink letting water run out the drain. In the sink, somewhere in the rushing water, was a translucent grape and she was trying to capture it before it went down the drain. In the peculiar values of dreams the grape was more valuable than a pearl. Almost than life itself; and frantically, though no one else in the kitchen had guessed her panic, she tried to cup the elusive grape in her calm hands. . . .

"I dreamed last night . . ." she begins and Nola who is fascinated by dreams holds still, the coffeepot in one hand, and listens to the dream with a face as blank and flittingly troubled as the face of a dreamer. Nola's free hand cups the grape in sympathy with the dream woman.

"I wouldn't want me a dream like that," she says after considerable reflection. She shakes the dream from her head and ears. "No sir-ree. . . ."

"Why?" Mrs. Perry asks.

"I just wouldn't," Nola says. "That's all."

Mrs. Perry knows she must allow Nola her time of mystery which may be five minutes or half the day before pressing for an answer.

"I don't think it means anything," Mrs. Perry says. She is looking out the window: "I thought I staked those peavines."

"They grow fast," Nola says as Mrs. Perry walks onto the side porch. The peas are a concession to the Depression. Vegetables are appearing now among the flowers: radishes in the petunias, carrots and parsley with the summer-snow, turnip greens beyond the alyssum.

Mrs. Perry walks down the gravel drive, through the iron gateway to the front yard. Here under the water oaks there is not yet a breeze and the fragrance of wisteria binding the porch is too heady, almost nauseating. She retreats to the gravel drive and back yard again. The coffee is undrinkable. She sets the cup on the porch and wonders why she feels so strongly the approach of a visitor.

She makes out a list in her head for the day: the twins, Moore to his music lesson, Marcia to tennis and the library. That gets the twins out of the way for the afternoon. She'll keep the little ones with her, sweeping the front walk and porch, running the wax mop over the dark, stained floors. She glances up at the peeling paint on the house. She has saved $83 to have it painted, and Mr. John Brown will scrape and paint it and repair the sagging steps, side and back, and repair all broken gutters and window cords for $125. He has come back last week and agreed since money is now so hard to come by, to do it for one hundred even, same paint, two coats like he said. But she feels $125 was the set price and intends to pay him that. The poor man has begged and she has finally agreed to pay in installments. When she has saved $100 he can commence; and she will pay him the $25 later. He wants to start immediately but they both know the $17 is not going to be easy to save. And in case of sickness which costs money, she will not be obliged to him.

Douglas Perry and Deliah were born in the house, in the very bed where her four children were born and Mrs. Perry loves the place. She makes no changes in it. All she does in the way of spending is for replacing (velvet draperies in the parlor, wooden blinds across the front); or for refinishing (floors scraped, brass chandeliers and brass doorknobs and name plate and numerals polished and reshellacked); or restoring (ivy pulled off the brick retaining walls and walks, trees pruned back, daisies planted to hide the legginess of the old shrubbery, rehanging the iron gates). Douglas and Deliah are amused by her respect for the place. But even they are becoming proud of it again. Now Marcia is taking an interest and before fall the tennis court may again have lines on it and a net of sorts. The Depression may last a lifetime but there is no excuse, she feels lately, in letting it depress children. Lately she has felt strong and her voice, she hopes, has that calm, confident tone of Roosevelt's. If she can make Douglas have faith in himself and his own strength! He and

Deliah used to be the ones with a real joy about them. Well, Deliah, in spite of Claude's death, still has. And Douglas has when Deliah is there and the children; but at night she sometimes has to hold him very tight and even then in his silences he seems to tremble. She has been poor almost all her life, but Douglas is not used to it. "What about the children?" he asks.

"I'd rather bring them up poor and with manners than running wild, rich." She is not criticizing his upbringing, because no family in town was ever more conservative and deliberately inconspicuous than his. She herself was taught by her mother to be proud poor, and with good manners and morals, the two were inseparable and rightly so.

"You can make up for having no garnets and sapphires by the way you hold your head and speak and move your hands," Mamma said when they complained. People who didn't know them thought from the balance of their heads, the steadiness of their eyes (not stating, simply not seeing) that they were haughty and were always delighted to hear the rich, but well modulated laughter which could come from the long throats of the Phillips girls. "You can judge a person by the way he laughs and by the way he accepts gifts." Mrs. Perry could hear her mother's voice. "And women, you can judge how they respect themselves by the way they respect their hair. Let a man not shave and let a woman not tend to her hair and you may know they are headed for trouble." Trouble, why was hers breaking now and coming out in such drifts?

Mrs. Perry begins the rhythmic strokes. She seizes the great cataract of hair at the scalp and draws her left hand, which barely reaches around the coil, slowly down it. The right hand with the British brush follows close behind and as the right hand reaches the tip, the left has already gathered the hair springing from the scalp and is drawing it again into an abundant rope. Again the brush starts at the nape of her neck, comes over the crown, and down the long, constrained rope of hair. Over and over until the rhythm is hypnotic. Occasionally she loses balance and tips forward toward the black taffeta square, but her body has the strength and skill of a dancer's and without a change in rhythm she straightens herself, and continues in the rhythm that soothes her mind and body.

She claims an hour to herself and is lucky to be granted thirty minutes. But some days for an hour she is allowed to return to the center of her being, to refind herself, to gather herself and her strength together, to be for one continuous time not. . . .

"Mama." The door is pushed open. Hannah, her baby girl, is standing there, at three already apologetic in a nice way, not cowering, simply aware she is intruding but feeling too strongly the need to. Hannah smiles winningly and when the smile is not returned she knows this is her mother's time to herself, thinks hard for something to say.

The mother holds back the weight of the hair with her entire forearm and looks under the arc at the child. "Yes, Hannah." Later she will be warm with the girl, make up for her coolness now.

Hannah has found something to say: "I think Baby Brother's awake."

She must be firm with Hannah even though Hannah has thought of such a charming story to gain admission. "No, Hannah, I don't think the baby is awake." Baby Brother is the new name for Hannah's soldier doll.

"I think he needs you." Hannah continues as if her story has not been refuted.

"Maybe the baby girl does," the mother smiles at her, "not the baby boy."

Hannah is ready, almost on tiptoes, to run to her and squeeze the life out of her with love. Of all the children Hannah is the one who can wreck herself each day with some emotion too strong for her young soul to bear.

"Mother will be out soon. You and Cindy keep clean."

Cindy, six, is standing now behind Hannah. Cindy is the little mother. If they are not shooed from the room, Cindy will find excuses to be in, straightening the bureau, making a great fuss over the tangle-balls of hair on the bureau, finding some excuse to be maid to her mother, to get her hands on the comb and brush. Today she is too tired to let Cindy even try to brush her hair, no, that would make her too nervous, today. Cindy refuses to have her own hair trimmed and already has demanded a comb and brush for Christmas. But Cindy's hair-brushing is at night and she still needs her mother's help with it. She considers it only fair play to help her mother in return.

"If you want to help me," the mother says, "see that you and Hannah stay clean till they get here."

"Can we help Nola?" Cindy is at the stage where it is hard to keep her out from under foot in the kitchen. Later when she is as old as Marcia and can be of help, she, like Marcia, will find excuses to go to the library, knowing that an education will take precedence over any domestic emergency.

"Nola is in the yard," the mother says. "In the yard" means resting, for it is under the fig tree that Nola has her own outdoor sitting room: two rush-bottomed chairs and a wicker bench. Here near the back gate she can receive visits from other cooks and nursemaids, and occasionally delivery boys. Their voices are part of the summer music and soothe the household. Baby-sitting is not part of Nola's rest period, for if the mother recognizes the need for an hour to herself, she demands it for Nola too. How long they can continue to pay Nola she does not know and Nola will not listen to any talk that she should accept other offers.

"Can we go visit Nola?" the children want to know.

"Did she invite you?"

"Yes!" Hannah lies immediately, joyfully, now that the idea has been invented.

Cindy, though older, is confused by Hannah's outright lie: "Not exactly. She doesn't know we want to see her."

The mother punishes them both with a short glance. "If she didn't invite you, you can't go."

The children seem smaller after her admonishment and she will later make lemonade for them if there is time but there probably will not be. She bends to her brushing again and is dizzy. She shuts her eyes to still the carpet.

"You go only where you are invited and you stay for meals if you are invited the day before." They are her words, her mother's words, her grandmother's words and are worn smooth by three generations of use. Even Hannah sometimes mocks her with them, behind her back to be sure, and she is pleased not annoyed when Hannah does. What you teach a child before it is five. . . .

"The guineas, the guineas are laying somewhere," Ardella's mother says. They have eaten lunch at the iron table built around the trunk of the cherry tree; for now while the tree is in bloom, and later in leaf shade through the heat of summer, they will picnic here at noon.

Her mother's words mean no more to Ardella than the clucking of the brood hen, the laughter of the ducks, the song of the morning-glory. Mockingbird, if she stops she knows morning-glory from mockingbird but the song is both. Her mother's words are repeated by her mother again; and again by Ardella's own silent lips but she is no longer eating buttered corn bread, she is standing in front of the furniture store in town five miles away and staring at the doll, a Confederate soldier. Ardella owns no real doll. Cindy is a sock-doll stuffed with cotton from the old Phillips plantation. . . .

"Mother, can we have . . ." the real Cindy speaks still, thirty years later, at the door. Listen to the needs of children, not to the words but what is actually being asked for ". . . one piece of gingerbread each."

"One piece each and that's all." They must learn the meaning of privacy; and for themselves, later, the need for it. "And shut the door now, Cindy, Hannah."

"Who is coming?" Cindy asks for the tenth time that day.

"I really don't know," the mother says. "If no one else, your Aunt Deliah."

"And Uncle Claude!" Hannah cries.

"Uncle Claude is dead!" Cindy says in horror. At six she does not understand death any better than does Hannah but she has learned in three months not to mention him, especially in front of Aunt Deliah.

"Uncle Claude will be here!" Hannah announces emphatically.

"Mother!" Cindy needs help or she may be convinced by Hannah.

"Children," the mother says, "shut the door."

She can hear the children explaining to each other the realities of their beliefs as they go down the long back stairs to the butler's pantry.

Hannah! One might as well argue with a gatepost, persuade a turnip. The poor man was not two days in his grave before she'd named her boy doll "Uncle Claude." Quite by chance she discovered she can say "Uncle Claude" if she claims it is her khaki doll she's talking about. But recently the doll has become "Baby Brother" and the mother hopes the name will last for the duration of Deliah's visit this evening.

The small dressing room, with the door to the bedroom shut, seems unduly hot and to open the outside door to the sleeping porch is to invite not only heat from the late afternoon sun but also more demands, from Nola, the twins, even from her husband should he have received her message at his office and arrived home early in anticipation of a guest who might turn out to be nothing more than—her own desire for company, her instinct telling her everyone needs a small party at the end of this particularly humid and tiring week tinged with growing poverty? She says to herself:

"Poor . . ." but before she knows what she intends to think, the heat, the closeness of the room has felled her and she is on all fours, crouched over the black taffeta, now a prayer rug. For a moment she must lie down.

She shuts her eyes and the street traffic is as distant and soft as wind in a forest and the back gate swinging idly on its hinges sings like, she knows but does not want to know . . . why can't Nola be persuaded to latch it after herself . . . sings like . . . a nausea threatens her throat and she shuts her eyes . . . Nola, latch the gate, the gate, latch it for God's sake . . . sings like . . . it's too late, let it swing, let it sing . . . like the rattlesnake. . . .

She is lying under the brush pile now and before her are the guinea eggs, a hundred of them, a thousand. Already she has filled her apron with the ones from the near edge but as far as she can see under the brush pile are eggs, eggs, and more eggs. Small brown guinea eggs. For each dozen her mother will give her a nickel and for twenty dozen a dollar. And for a dollar the Confederate doll will be hers to take out of the store window, to hold on the way home, sitting on her pillow on the back of the wagon.

"Mamma," she wants to scream, "Mamma, I've found

where the guinea hens are laying." But her mother with her two baskets, one for wild strawberries, one for mushrooms, has long ago disappeared into the forest and young ladies do not scream. She tries to count the eggs but they come together, double, treble, she counts the same egg twice and pretends not to notice the hissing is growing stronger and stronger. First it is far away, then it is near. Now it is everywhere. As if each egg is singing a dry rattling song.

She knows the noise; she knows what it means. Yet by an order to herself, she does not look away from the eggs which she is reaching for as far as her ten-year-old summer-brown arms will reach. She crawls deeper under the brush. She follows her hands gathering the eggs as if her hands were kittens to be sneaked up on, caught, dragged back to her bosom. And all the time the silky sliding rattle which she orders herself not to hear.

She sees the doll in the store window; she sees herself holding it on the wagon; she cannot quite see herself with the doll at home, in the house. On the porch she sees herself hiding there with the doll, waiting behind the boxwoods for the Yankees, the Cherokees, for all mortal enemies, she and the soldier protecting them all from all evil.

Again she slides forward, dragging carefully the apron-bag by its neck. Now she is under the center of the brush pile and one way out is as short as another. Above the eggs, above the place where she sees the doll in the window, and on the porch a branch creaks heavily, something heavy drops to a lower branch, the pile shifts and seems all to move. The silky droning stops then starts again, moving slowly as the brush pile seems to slide. She is looking into the eyes of the snake itself, nearer, ever nearer, till death do us part. Her hands move out again, toward the eggs, obeying again the unvoiced command from that unknown part of her which will have the doll at any price. Two more eggs, two more. The head of the snake weaves from side to side. The thick body coils through the brush toward the nest. Now it is a moral battle: the eggs must be rescued, saved from the snake. Now the eggs have the love withdrawn from the soldier doll. Now she is a mother rescuing her young from all terror. Two more eggs and two more and the snake has reached the far edge of the nest and dangles its head above the eggs. Cautiously, two more and she will crawl backward, and drag the apron-bundle of eggs after her, and place them safely near the spring and run to her mother, slowing to a ladylike walk, where the mother is kneeling ladylike, bending at the knees, not from the waist, turning the perfect leaves, picking the little berries which will be served with sugar tonight. Approaching softly saying softly, "Mamma, I have found the guinea nest where the guinea hens are laying. Saturday when we go to town, I will have money. . . ." No snake. No. No snake. No.

The darting tongue flickers, fast as a bee wing, the head holds still, the thick body begins its coil for strength and spring. Two more eggs. That is enough. That is enough. Twice more the hands go out and twice more back and are moving forward again when the snake strikes and misses, its thick body smashing the eggs, thrashing over the broken eggs, through the brush.

Back, back, she scrambles back screaming without a sound from her dry lips. No snake. No. She is out from under the brush. No snake. No. She is running. No snake. She has the apron with her and the eggs are dropping out one by one. No. She holds them to her bosom and saves them. No snake. Blind with panic she has entered the woods, and blind and deaf she is when she walks into her strolling mother. No. No. No. Now, for the first time she breathes.

The picture is gone and under her on the floor is the black taffeta. The ivory handle of the brush is wet in her hand. She cannot push herself back to her kneeling position. For a moment, only for a moment longer she will lie here on the floor. The children cannot see her and will not be tempted to copy her. She is thankful for the thick carpet under her and feels better. The dizziness passes and with it all further knowledge of that day some thirty years before. Did she get the doll? She cannot remember it if she did. She seems to remember looking at it again in the store window and thinking: "It is not the same doll." They cannot persuade her to buy it. It is not at any rate the doll her heart was set on.

Or is she confusing herself with Hannah and the khaki soldier doll? Hannah drags it around and has no maternal feeling for it at all. No, if she had got a doll she would have loved it and remembered it. Maybe there had not been money enough for them to buy the eggs. Or to please them she had said she no longer wanted the doll she, before, had wanted more than anything in the world.

Now the twins are back from music and the library. Moore is at the piano, the music bench slams shut; half-heartedly he runs a scale and midway breaks into a hymn and from there a waltz. Marcia is hitting a tennis ball against the side of the carriage house, mainly to annoy Nola on the other side, who is hollering at her to desist. Those two and their arguing, she is not sure she can take much of it this summer.

The horn of the A-model sounds in the shady back street and the gravel sprays as he turns, as usual, too fast into the driveway. "Douglas, one of these days a child is going to be playing there and you. . . ."

But now she must get up. It is as if she had been asleep in the hammock and is stiff from cold. She rolls over on the floor and rises unsteadily to her feet. Already so late. Douglas home. Maybe the visitor is with him.

"Aunt Deliah! Deliah!" First Hannah begins and then the others, even the twins. Already before Deliah is out of the car it is a party. There'll be something, if no more than a balloon for every one of them, including Nola and Douglas and herself. Deliah never forgets anyone. A constrictor of jealousy tightens for only a second around her heart as she glances from the sleeping porch and sees Deliah being pulled by not one but all the children. It is a game and even Douglas laughs as he tries to rescue his sister. Ardella has forgotten Douglas's laugh, she hears it so seldom lately. Tonight though will be a party!

With the children diverted and Douglas and Deliah together, she takes her time dressing. Dressed, and with a linen towel about her shoulders, she coils the hair about her wrist and lets it slip over her head to be pinned with large celluloid pins to the crown of her head. She studies her face, glowing from heat and the exertion of arranging her hair, and thinks how strange that only a few minutes before she was lying on the floor in her dressing shift. She gathers the cloud of hair and rolls it into a ball before letting it float into the wicker basket.

She stands too quickly and the blood leaves her head. She reaches for the door to the bedroom and unsteadily approaches the bed. "I'll lie down, just for a second," she thinks, and when she opens her eyes again the room is darker, the house quieter. She has dozed off and now is waking.

Moore and Deliah are playing a duet. She listens. No, how strange: it is not Moore; it is Douglas and Deliah. As she listens a peace, deeper than any she has known for a long time, fills her as she lies there. ". . . Gone are the cares from life's early toil . . ." now their voices rise to her. On the side porch the children are whispering, plotting some mischief for the table. The children move off to plot with Nola on the back porch; and downstairs the singing breaks off and only one person, Douglas, begins an etude, simply, lightly, as if his mind is on a hummingbird.

Ardella rises carefully and this time is not made dizzy by standing. She reaches the top step and, lest the vertigo return, descends carefully the wide, carpeted front stairs. Before she is all the way down, she hears, not meaning to, Deliah's voice, rich and musical: "She's so beautiful when she's pregnant. I knew by her face, the glow. . . ."

Ardella pauses and automatically places a protective hand over her stomach. "Pregnant?" She feels herself flushing. The knowledge fills every cell of her body at once.

"Why hasn't she told me?" Douglas finds the right, light touch for each note. "It makes me. . . ."

"Jealous!" Deliah cries. "Oh Douglas! I know, I know!"

"How long . . . when?" the music falters, stops.

"I don't know. But the morning we buried Claude I knew by a grim, angry look about her face before a year she would have another, that she would replace Claude. There's a certain wonderful type of woman who will always fight death with birth."

For an instant Ardella is tempted to flee back upstairs; but thinks incongruously, her hand still on her stomach: "There goes the house paint. Poor Mr. Brown. No. I promised him and I will." How? Why must they always guess before she allows herself to know? How long has she known without admitting it? She must stop them from saying more.

"Deliah!" she calls. "Douglas, didn't I promise you we'd have company today? Deliah. . . ." With arms outstretched, her heart bursting with love for her widowed sister-in-law, her husband, the children, Nola, the entire vulnerable world, she enters the parlor.

And I, the dreamer, yet unborn, her last child, the unannounced guest, enter the room with her, having finally been allowed to share that hour of privacy which later was always denied to me when she brushed her hair.

Now, SITTING here at my desk, I am confused. For the gate in the story is the iron gate my wife has just had repaired here in San Francisco; and the dressing room is not in the house where I grew up but here in this house where once in play I surprised my wife (my mother, my child); and the party—I begin to understand.

Again I return to the night of our party. Howie and I stood up, still talking, and I opened the door to the living room. At the far end, between the candelabra on the low piano, Kathy and Eve, their fingers racing in a childish duet, were laughing when they glanced up at us.

At the moment I guessed from Kathy's radiance that she had told Eve her news; and I was merely feeling glad I had not mentioned to Howie anything about a baby. It seemed right it should be the news of women.

But now in memory, I stand there in awe; for I am the son who gained access to the dressing room; and I am the father who admitted jealousy of that son, who am I standing at the door, looking toward another unborn son (my father to be reborn?), who, too, am I; for I am the snake and the egg, the creator and the created; for I am the dreamer.

Forget the Geraniums

WE WERE sitting as usual that summer on the terrace of the Café Mona, around the corner from the Odéon and straight down from the Comédie Française. Now it was late August and the streets were deserted. Thousands of Parisians had gone south on their annual holidays and the only creature about was the street-cleaner with his broom of bound twigs.

Benito Rapello—an American artist studying on the GI Bill—and I were alone on the terrace that morning. The fact is he had sent me a *pneumatique* asking me to meet him here. The note was rather puzzling because I did not really know him that well: I had seen him several times in an evening sketching class and later had gone with Daphne, a mutual friend, to the opening of his third exhibit, which was even more successful (the French liked it, that is) than the first two; and I had talked with him maybe ten times in passing on the street.

He was about thirty, extremely clean-cut and perhaps too good-looking in a Latin way: teeth too regular and white, eyes too dark and soft, a strong jaw too square, complete in every way, even down to the cleft chin and jaw muscle which rolled and dimpled when he chewed or talked. Sometimes he was with a strikingly beautiful woman but I think there was nothing to that because she was living with a sculptor in Montparnasse.

Usually he was alone and always in a hurry, which was understandable considering the fact that he had over sixty paintings in each show and all three in a period of four years. Solid clean water colors of the Seine, quite simple and nice and unpretentious; and even more solid oils which were of Paris too, places one knew quite well, such as the bridge at St. Martin or the *quais* along the Île St. Louis, but which in his pictures were the most desolate places in the world, filled with a solemn green light which one might expect to see in the sky in advance of a hurricane or maybe thirty minutes after an atomic blast. It was this strange, impending, doomed light and the complete bareness and lack of hope, that the French liked and not the admirable draftsmanship which they looked upon with contempt as at anything out-dated in the fields of fashion and ideas. The other American GI students were guardedly quite proud of him, in spite of a certain envy—not of his paintings, they let you know—but of his ability to work, and work hard and stay out of café life. As a result there were rumors about him of various sorts, so contradictory that if you considered them all together they seemed rather ridiculous. If he were aware of these rumors one could never know: he was always very pleasant, though extremely serious, polite, correct, even a little formal. Certainly he dressed more like a bright young man just out of Harvard than like a Left Bank artist or an American student in Paris.

Well then, he was sitting at the Café Mona that morning when I arrived at ten o'clock. The place was naturally deserted at that early hour, it being mainly a nighttime hangout for the odd assortment of strange Americans and their tobacco-hungry, occasional admirers. His blue-black beard, more like a thick paste than like a stubble, would have been surely an affectation, a rather silly source of pride for a vain man, but he stroked it immediately and apologized for it by saying that he had been up all night and had not been home to shave. Otherwise he looked, as always, quite neat and healthy. He ordered a coffee and croissant for me but wanted nothing himself. During the time Pierre had gone to fetch the coffee and bun I said without too much curiosity: "I haven't seen you around in a long time. Not since the beginning of summer, isn't it?"

"Yes," he said. "At least two months." He paused as though that would be all, then wet his thin lips, which were already wet, with the tip of his tongue and let them curl ironically. "I've been crucifying Christ."

"Crucifying Christ," I said as though it might be a well-known expression or joke, if it were a joke.

"No, quite seriously. I've been nailing Christ to the cross."

"For two months?" I asked. "Is it a painting?"

"No. I had to get a job. My GI Bill ran out in June and I went down to a foundry a French friend works summers in—where they're casting those warhorses for Perén, as a matter of fact—and got a job nailing Christ to the cross. I had to have work." He explained that they made every size crucifix. From pocket size to cathedral size. Stacks and stacks of them. All day long. He sighed suddenly and all the irony drained from his face, leaving his eyes unusually dark. "Well, it's over now."

"Uh-oh," I thought warily. "He wants to borrow money. Why else a *pneumatique* at nine in the morning?" All the broke Americans assumed they could borrow money from anyone who still wore a tie and socks.

He may have seen the close, guarded look on my face for he added: "I quit."

That did not make the possibility of a loan less likely. But then he said, flatly, in exactly the same tone as before: "I'm going to kill myself."

"I beg your pardon," I said. It was probably another expression, like Crucifying Christ, which too would have a perfectly plausible, unalarming explanation.

He looked up from the water running along the curb and for a second his face tightened so that he did not need to add another word for emphasis; but he did, nevertheless, calmly and flatly as before: "I'm going to kill myself."

It would have been too dramatic, indeed burlesque, to set the coffee cup down noisily on the saucer, so I took a long sip while trying to think. When I could delay no longer and it was obvious that he had nothing more to say, I asked: "Do you know why?"

HE KNEW why. That was a little after ten o'clock and at a little after three he was still orating why. He was not sad. It was no momentary depression. It was something he had been considering sanely for some time, even before coming to Europe. It was not love, money, or success. It was not the lack of any of these three. He could have anything he wanted. He wanted nothing. "Everything is a farce," he kept saying in summation. No matter what we talked about he concluded that it was a farce.

Even so, to me after a night of sleep, that did not seem reason enough for suicide. It could as easily be the reason for trying to stay alive as long as possible. But I listened not so much to his words as to the flat tone in his voice and knew that he was not merely playing. Once you have heard that note, calm, beyond despair, you heed it when you hear it again a second time. In college I had known an unhumorous lad who said in that matter of fact voice that he was going to kill himself and who had gone straightway unheeded (it was during a football broadcast) to his room, poured lighter fluid over his clothes, set them on fire, cut his throat with a razor blade, and jumped out of the third floor of the dormitory onto the cement service platform. An ambulance could not be got so he had to be half-carried, half-walked, wrapped in a blanket, across the campus to the infirmary where he went into shock and died almost immediately. So here at the Café Mona I listened without alarm but with real respect to Benito Rapello's undramatic words which were convincing because of the complete lack of emotion with which he recited them.

One thing I kept in mind while he spoke: "He wants to be talked out of it, he wants to be persuaded. Otherwise he would have done it last night. Otherwise he would not have waited alone until the post office opened to send the note." I would have hoped for someone else to join us to aid, but we had only one friend in common, Daphne, and she was now in North Africa. Each time he stopped talking I would ask a question, for when the silence became too long and deep he always ended it by extending his hand and saying thanks for listening and moving in his chair as though about to leave. It didn't seem a good idea to be persuading him constantly to stay or to live because if he kept pretending or threatening he would have both to leave and to kill himself for his own distorted pride.

"But your painting?" I said tentatively, knowing that it sounded fatuous to a man who had been up all night and got himself into such a state.

"To hell with it," he said.

"But the reviews were excellent. Even Bernard Mérimée's."

"Exactly," he said. "But what does it mean? I can paint. I know that. I can go on and on and paint more and more pictures and better and better and better ones and the critics will say more and more decent things and stupid people will start buying them and paying more and more. But what does it come to? Nothing. It's a farce. A great big farce like everything else." We talked about painting for almost forty minutes: the young painters who were being pushed by the right critics; those who had real talent who were building respectable reputations; those who were phonies who were getting there on exploitable personalities; those who were arriving by affording chic galleries; those who had once had talent but who now, having nothing more to say, were turning out slick phony junk and becoming even more the rage; those who were willing to pay actual money to critics. All these people arriving, getting there, some through merit, some not, but all arriving. And where was there? It was a great big farce; that's what it was, a farce.

"What about going back to the States?" I offered. But no, he had left the States with exactly this same sense of futility, not as acute and debilitating as now because then he had believed that the fault lay not within himself but in the essentially materialistic, essentially anti-intellectual philosophy of the Americans. Now he knew that was not true. Their ambitions were simply different, their goals perhaps more obvious and less admirable (to own a Packard rather than a Picasso), their means more direct and open. But even so, here or there it was a farce.

For a while, his first year abroad, he had not understood America and had been in constant revolt against its mania for cleanliness and against its puritanism. He had grown a beard, gone dirty, worn clothes that hung like rags. He had slept with so many that he sometimes did not recognize them any longer on the street. All in meaningless revolt against a meaningless system. Farce in reaction to farce.

"Women," he said. "I've had more women in two years here than I would have thought possible. Sometimes serious affairs too, but they always end the same way: boredom. No, seriously," he said when he saw my quizzical brow. "After a while anything becomes boring and I don't think I'm capable of any real, deep, sustaining emotion, except in painting." He paused a long time, then said without any vanity but as a statement of ordinary fact: "You can't look like me," he indicated his face with a flare of his hand, "and have a straight back, strong chest, no hips, and good legs without attract-

ing more women than you know what to do with. And men.
And I've tried that but it's ridiculous." He had tried, it
evolved, beer, wine, reefers, cognac, complete celibacy, and
every other vice, and having a completely detached approach
was not at all interested in what anyone said. "Those petty
little gossipers see all those things, like drunkenness and lust-
ings, as ends in themselves rather than as ways toward something real: as a way out of oneself." But now he was tired of
experimenting, tired of trying to break through his isolation.

DURING THESE long discourses I was trying to remember
articles on suicide I had read since the night the stunned boy
had been found on the dormitory step and led dazed and
pleading to the infirmary. ("No one believed me," he kept
saying, his eyes wide and wild, "no one believed me." And
then lying on the floor in the hall of the infirmary whispering from his torn-looking mouth: "If you only knew what it
is I'm afraid of." What it was he never revealed.) More people, I remembered, kill themselves in daytime than at night,
more on sunny than on dark days, more on Sundays and
holidays than during work days. None of this was encour-
aging for here we sat in the middle of a bright sunny afternoon while half of Paris was away on holidays. People rarely
kill themselves, the book had said, on a full stomach, but
Benito Rapello refused any invitation to go around the cor-

ner to a restaurant. He had a cup of tea before him only because Pierre, the waiter, insisted that he could not sit there all day without ordering. The fragrance of geraniums, a professor had said, was known to have an exhilarating effect upon depressed patients, but he had not explained how to lead the patient to a geranium.

Finally I asked what I had been wondering since receiving his note: "Why me? Why did you decide to talk first to me?" It sounded blunt and even accusing, but he did not seem to notice.

"Because," he said, "Daphne told me that you tried to commit suicide."

"Did she?" I was astonished. I could not even remember having confided such information to her. Actually I was annoyed.

"Yes," he continued. "Oh, it was nothing. I'd merely mentioned that you, more than most people here, seemed to know what you were doing and apparently enjoyed being alive. She said maybe so but you'd poured lighter fluid on yourself in college and jumped from a window."

"That was somebody else." I reddened disagreeably. "A boy I knew."

He watched the red which would not subside and half-relenting, half-persisting said: "Maybe I got the story wrong. But you have tried?"

He had no right to be asking, but then under the circumstances I had no right to refuse him any knowledge that might change his mind.

"I suppose most people have. Or have thought about it."

"But you almost succeeded." He obviously believed I was the lad with the lighter fluid.

"Yes." I said and felt, under his gaze, that I should lean casually over and turn the water on the table before us into wine. Such desperate faith he had in me now: how could I admit that I had merely swallowed forty-four of what were supposed to be powerful sleeping pills and then had (for fifteen dollars) rushed myself to the hospital in an ambulance to have them pumped out? Or about the laughter of the intern who discovered, in such a loud voice, that it had been only milk of magnesia tablets? Under Benito's admiring gaze I sat discreetly trying to look like one who had been burned, slashed, and hurled from a third floor window.

"What made you change your mind?" he asked. "You seem happy enough now."

I shrugged my shoulders and pouted like a Frenchman. Such a complex question that any answer would be silly, incomplete, and untruthful. "Analysis, I suppose."

"Psychoanalysis!" he spit the word out as though it were fat meat.

I admitted reluctantly yes, wondering, with annoyance,

why in hell some people can't kill themselves without having to ask personal questions.

HE BEGAN a tremendous, offensive tirade against analysis,
so bitter that I knew he was extremely interested. I said nothing and made no defenses for it. In fact I agreed with him
on many points: it was painfully expensive, and did certainly
take time, sometimes years; yes, some people seemed not to
benefit outwardly from it, though you couldn't be sure they
were dismissed. The only positive point I insisted on was
that it was a wiser choice than suicide. He argued on and on
but always we came back to the fact which I established with
authority: it was a wiser choice than suicide. Finally and
quite suddenly he agreed by saying: "Do you know of any
psychiatrist here? One who speaks English."

"If I do, will you go?"

He thought for several minutes. "For how long?"

"For even one hour."

Again he reflected: "Yes, for one hour."

"You'll wait here?" I asked without stressing the question.
"While I phone."

He said sure.

I phoned the American Hospital and asked for a list of
psychiatrists who spoke English. The girl there explained
that many of the doctors were out of town during the holi-

days. Couldn't I telephone back in September? When I told her my predicament she let me speak at once to a neurologist on duty who said I didn't want to get in touch with an analyst but with a psychiatrist and gave me immediately the name and address of one with whom he had talked only five minutes before and who fortunately lived not ten minutes' walk from the Café Mona, three minutes by cab. He himself would telephone the man that we were on the way. Well naturally he couldn't say but he didn't think Rapello would do anything drastic, not if he had been sitting talking rationally all day, but he shouldn't go, in such a state, alone through another night without sleep.

We walked. Rapello wanted to buy cigarettes. He considered, too, going to his room to shave which could have been a hopeful sign or merely a ruse, so we went on without stopping. All the way he became more nervous: "What am I going to say to the man?"

"Just what you've been saying to me."

"Just that?" He stopped. "What's the use of going?"

"He may ask you a few questions. May ask you something which will open up whole new fields of thinking, whole new ways of looking at yourself and at the world."

Rapello was not convinced but he followed and as we rang the bell to the heavy door he whispered like a child: "All that I said this morning to you?"

"Whatever you like," I whispered back.

Suddenly he drew away. "About the money. I don't have any with me. How much is this going to cost?"

"He won't ask for money. If he does I have some."

The doctor himself opened the door and the girl at the desk in the reception room did not even look up from her typing. A rather elegantly dressed lady sat nervously pretending to read a magazine which she had obviously just picked up. The doctor regarded us and could not make up his mind. Had my mask of sanity slipped?

"This is Benito Rapello," I said hastily in introduction. "The American Hospital called you about an appointment, didn't they?"

"Yes, yes," he said kindly but rather vaguely. "Fortunately I have some minutes." He had a very heavy accent, clearly not French, perhaps German or farther east even. He chose his words with careful deliberation, like a near-sighted typesetter, as though he were not sure they were the words he wanted.

Rapello disappeared with him into the tremendous Louis Quinze living room beyond the sliding doors. The nervous patient glanced at her watch and said in a torrent of French that she could not sit here like this, that she would come back in thirty minutes, in an hour, never if she felt like it. The girl did not look up from her typing during this outpour or when the door slammed shut.

Beyond the sliding door Benito Rapello's steady voice droned on, five minutes, ten, fifteen, a half an hour, forty-five minutes. During this time I went over all that he had said that morning and hoped the wise-looking old doctor could find a more appropriate comment than I had found. ("But I'm simple," I had said lamely, yet sincerely. "I like farce.") Near the end of the hour the girl asked Rapello's name, address, and ability to pay which she typed onto a card.

WHEN THE sliding doors finally opened and the two came into the room, Rapello's eyes were as happy and bright as a child's but the doctor's face was as before: calm, sage, and inscrutable. Rapello thanked the doctor and as he did so his face broke into an amused smile, the sparkle and sincerity of which completely startled me. He was almost laughing. When the old doctor opened the door, Rapello burst out, and, most unlike him, galloped down the steps. He raced through the hall below too fast for me to keep up.

"Wait. Hey, wait up!" For a moment I didn't know whether to follow or go back and call for the doctor. When I caught up with him at the corner he turned, as though still unaware of me, toward the Seine.

"What did he say?"

But Benito was across the street and off again toward the river. We were almost running now and when I came abreast of him his eyes were still bright and his thin lips were twitching to hold back a grin. "Let's go get a beer," he said. "I'll buy you one."

NEAR THE Beaux Arts we sat in front of a café looking out across at the Louvre. We were both breathing hard and Benito had not yet decided to relate what had happened in the conference room. He merely sat shaking his head from side to side and the smile was growing into a broad grin.

"Well," I said when the waiter had placed the beers before us and left.

"I talked for an hour . . ." Rapello began chuckling. "I talked for an hour. . . ." Handsome people rarely give themselves over to any emotion so disfeaturing and contorting as open laughter; but for a second Benito Rapello threatened to. Long habit though straightened his face and smoothed his features again. "I told him just what I told you this morning: everything is a farce."

"Yes?" I said in mock-sobriety.

"He just sat there listening." Benito's lips began stretching into an elastic grin that would not stay the same size. "Not saying a word. Only listening. And nodding his head in agreement."

Benito drank off half his beer as though he were just back from a three-day desert journey. "He didn't say a word. Not until the end of the hour."

"What then?"

For a moment Benito could do nothing with the grin. But finally he said: "At the end of the hour, he reached for an English dictionary on his desk and said: 'This word: *farce*. What does it mean?'"

That was almost a year ago. Now when Benito Rapello and I meet on the street or see each other on the terrace of the Café Mona he says: "This word, farce." And I say: "What does it mean, Lazarus?"

The Man in the Doll House

"I ALWAYS thought," he said to Oakley, "when you go back to a place everything is supposed to look smaller than you remembered." For the past three years his son had had so little to say to him that he had taken to thinking aloud, no longer in the hopes of engaging the boy's interest.

The campus, the entire town of Chapel Hill had never been lovelier. The leaves were, as Willa Cather had said about another place in the same season, "no larger than squirrels' ears" and there was a green haze over all the trees. "Everything is larger." It was not just an illusion: the stadium had new tiers; the chemistry building had a tower that totally dwarfed the old building; and the swimming pool had been replaced by two twice the size of the one where one summer he had spent dangerously hot afternoons as a lifeguard.

Now standing before the old wing of the Inn, the middle-aged man, thick but not yet heavy, and his tall skinny son had stopped for the traffic light. "Huge," he said. "I'd like to see it from a helicopter. Everything is much larger."

"Maybe it's you that's gotten smaller," the boy said, not quite sullenly but certainly not pleasantly enough for it to be a joke.

Well, he had. As a lifeguard he had stood six feet two inches. Now he wondered if he were even six feet. Here Oakley, only eighteen, was taller, even the way he stood with his shoulders rounded, neck bent, looking at the ground as if the answers to his misery lay somewhere near his feet, enormous in their torn Adidas.

"It happens," he said. "I was your age . . ." but he had told him that on the plane coming down from Virginia. Just out of the Korean War, ". . . a little older." The admission officer in 1955 had said he could be admitted but warned that there were no rooms available. "That's why I go back to see Shardey every time I'm here." He could never tell if the boy was listening. Until one of them got angry. "Look," he said. "Your appointment is at four." He pointed down the hill to the Health Complex which began at the foot and sprawled over the entire next hill. It had been one building his senior year. "It'll be hard to find the psychiatric center and his office. He advised giving yourself thirty minutes. . . ."

"I can find it," the boy said.

"Are you going to change clothes?"

The boy looked down at his knit shirt from which he had carefully removed the alligator with a razor blade, at his jeans, slit at one knee, and at his sneakers. "I look the way I am. I hope he won't have the same values you do."

"Why are you angry?" he asked. "I buy you new clothes. I fly you down here. It wouldn't have occurred to my father to show me around a campus."

"What makes you think I'm angry?"

"I would never have spoken to my father in that tone."

"If you want me to be angry, I'll be angry." The boy was glaring at him. "All right. I am angry now. Is that what you wanted?"

For a moment he studied the boy's tight face and chewed on the inside of his own cheek before saying, quietly: "I'm not coming in. I'll be at Shardey's when you get back. Wait for me here or come on to Shardey's. She would like to meet you." He watched as the boy stalked across the street and up the horseshoe drive to the Inn. Maybe he'd been wrong to take the boy from his mother, but what hope was there for him in that godless house? "Oakley," he called, knowing it would embarrass him, "you've got the map to Shardey's?"

The boy nodded violently and with a brown bag under his arm the man went down the hill toward Westwood where Shardey lived. Rock walls followed the gravel walk past the fraternity houses and he remembered Oakley, two years old, walking on them, almost from his first steps, holding his hand or sometimes running on ahead to the next walkway where he would wait and then swing onto his father's neck to be carried to where the wall picked up again.

SHARDEY WAS strolling on her side verandah. "Time," she said managing in one gracious moment both to hold out her arms wide to him and to keep a paisley shawl about her shoulders. At least she was smaller than he had remembered, or was it the huge shawl that made her appear so? The shawl was the same one that always smelled so dusty draped over the closed curved top of the Steinway. He put the paper bag down before embracing her.

He held her close, the old woman softness, and felt with a shock the cold of her synthetic wig. She had strength enough to squeeze and so could not be failing as fast as he had heard. She prolonged the embrace and he waited for her to feel the moment was over, but she held on like a child who had waited, unbelieving, for his return. How safe he felt standing here giving her comfort and how frightened he would have been in his student days to allow her to hug him, when there were moments when he needed more than anything to be hugged by her or anyone. Now her arms were weakening, and still with no coy patting, but with dignity she was releasing him. For a moment they stood and looked at each other. It had been almost thirty years since he first stood here on the same spot to rent a room from her.

The room had turned out to be a doll house which ran the length of the garage and was maybe wide enough for a truck, large enough at least for a twin-size brass bed. The rest of the furniture was still doll furniture. Each drawer of the little stencilled chest had held one laundered shirt, each window seat one pair of army boots or sneakers. The little stove burned one head-size lump of coal, and among the books on the bookshelves above the casement windows were little painted tin tea sets that had belonged to Hillary.

"How is Hillary?" he asked, one arm still about her shoulder as she walked him through the glass door to the dark hall. It would be so easy for anyone to break a small pane of the door and turn the night latch.

"Married again. Of course," she said. "It's too boring. I'll tell you about it. Or maybe I won't."

He was studying her as they walked across the bright living room. After the initial shock (it had been six years since he had seen her and she would now be over eighty-five), she seemed much the same. Except for the sort of Bette Davis frosted wig which had bangs that looked as if she had tried shaping them with kitchen shears. A good ruddy Irish woman. Broad. Round-faced with white hairs sprouting out at all sorts of angles from her moles and chin and enough to cover solidly the space above her upper lip. A denim wrap-around skirt and some strange beaded moccasins which he was sure had a story as all her possessions had.

"Hillary knows nothing about men. That's why she keeps marrying them." They were now before the casement windows which ran across the back of the house and looked out on a lawn and on the tall shrubbery which hid his doll house. "But then how could she. . . ." Shardey had adopted three daughters. One at a time, she always explained. "I would get one as a baby and bring her up and get her through college and in the case of Cran through medical school, give her one year in Europe; and then get the next one. Then I would push them out. I always had to get on with the next one. Sixty years. More." All with no husband and apparently with no red tape from adoption agencies. She had searched them out as babies and brought them up. "How could she have known anything about marriage? How could she have known what sort of music men and women make together?"

He could not resist asking, but smiled when he did: "What kind of music do men and women make together?"

"Sacred. That's what kind. You think because I've never been married I don't know. Well, it's true, I always tried and thought I could sing both parts: that's what an egotist is. But how was Hillary to learn?" She stared at him as if she were going to ask: "And what kind of music did you and your wife make together?" Then something in her face relented. And what kind had they? Not a jolly song to be whistled, that was for sure.

"Now what are we going to drink?" she was asking, looking about the room as if she had left a bottle among the hanging ferns above the windows. She seemed a little anxious, maybe even disoriented as he had heard she sometimes was, and he was glad for the chance to go to the porch and get the sherry and cheese he had brought.

Outside the air was damp and clear and as far down the street as he could see the yards were dotted with jonquils in sudden bloom. For a moment he was hurt by the beauty of the place as much as he had been those first two years, during which any time he shut his eyes, day or night, he was back in Korea. (Now Oakley, looking and acting exactly like him, all locked into himself with no way to get out.)

As he started in he was surprised to see a middle-aged woman coming toward him across the lawn from the front steps. "Are you going to be with her for an hour or so? She said you would and I've got to get to the store and back." When he told her he would, she said, "It won't hurt for her to be by herself a few minutes if you have to leave. Somebody else is coming later. Some man from out of town."

He was angry to see she had a housekeeper and as he walked back into the house he realized it was because in his mind he had imagined Oakley living here, checking on her, helping with errands, somewhat as he had done.

"Yes," Shardey said standing in front of the stone fireplace staring at the brown bag. "Much better than tea." Above the mantel was a Flemish painting of the world. Of all her possessions, except perhaps the Oriental carpets, this was what he wished most she would give him when she made her frequent promises. "Good, but not better than tea," he said. No one had ever made better tea. His second year on rainy afternoons when she would catch him trying to sneak up the drive, unseen, she would make him come in and join her.

"We could have both," he said.

"You have tea. I'll have that good Scotch you always bring." He had never brought her Scotch.

"Sherry," he said.

"Same thing. Alcohol. Now let's go see what we can find in the way of tea and biscuits."

The kitchen had been newly tiled with Mexican tiles ("Cran last summer," she explained) but still he could smell the ghost of wet wooded drain boards, the roachy smell of cupboard shelves lined with yellowed copies of *The London Times*. It was clear she did not know what she was looking for in the kitchen and when she saw him watching her and aware of her confusion she exposed her strong yellow teeth in a smile like a baby's. "Lear, I always wanted to play Lear."

She had played Juliet's nurse in England. And the fall he was taking Shakespeare they had read the play together, she throwing herself across the lawn and posturing against trees, while he sat on the porch of the doll house which held, if not rocked, one wicker rocker. One London critic had said of her part: "A Miss Irene Shardey informs the role with new life, illuminating it with keen intelligence and a deep pathos. . . ." Sitting beside him on the stone wall by the doll house she had explained that she had known instinctively, because she had never seen her own mother, that of all the people in the world it was the nurse who knew Juliet best, who loved her most, even more than Romeo could ever possibly, and that here was no buffoon to be played for laughs, but a woman suffering to the bone and hiding it under a cockney accent. After a silence she had patted the stones and said, "No one ever had a bad conversation on a rock wall. They bring out the truth."

"I THOUGHT you were going to show me your son. Where's your son?" She had found the tea things all laid out in plain view on the table. Everything just the way he remembered: the orange Jug Town pots, the basket of imported dry crackers, unmatching fringed napkins. "Isn't this fun isn't this fun isn't this fun . . ." she was saying and humming. He would not tell her yet that Oakley might be in school and therapy here next year. He was not sure he believed in therapy but because he, himself, had been miserable here and gotten better here, he felt confident in something curative about the place.

He carried the tray with the brewing tea into the living room and at her direction placed it on the table before the slate hearth. "We don't need a fire, do we?" When she tilted her head toward the fireplace where the paper and kindling were ready to be lit, her wig slid over one eye. She pushed it back, too far, and he could see the wisps of fine white hair above her broad forehead. He was certain she should not have a fire going if he had to leave before someone else arrived. There was an extra cup on the tray. "You have too many cups," he said.

"Oh no, no. That's what I've been meaning to tell you. There is the most talented man coming this afternoon. I've always wanted to get you two together." She was famous for getting people together and no one was ever sure if she knew how awkward and sometimes disastrous the meetings were. She was fussing with the tray, saying under her breath, ". . . such fun such fun . . ." until he asked her who the man was who was coming.

"Oh, he's quite distinguished. Very well known. . . ."

He could tell she had gone completely blank and had no idea what this man was distinguished for. "In his field. You would recognize his name," she laughed a good hearty laugh, "if I could recall it. It makes me so angry not to be able to remember names. I can tell you everything about him. He was one of those people who live in the past because they don't have courage enough to face the future."

She leaned back among the pillows and then sat forward, pulling from behind her a drawstring bag. She looked at it as if it were something a stranger had slipped into the house and hidden there. Forgetting him she studied it and carefully opened it and rummaged inside. Her hand stopped and she looked up at him sadly, her wig still askew, but with real dignity in her face. "Did you ever wonder what I carried in my bag? My baskets, everyone knew what was in them. Food and flowers." Once she had said to him when he ran into her at the post office: "An old Irish woman can't go anywhere without her basket."

She stared at him now, deliberating whether to show him or not what she was holding in her hand inside the bag. Then she drew it out in a grand gesture. A crucifix. A gold Christ on a gold cross. Bigger than her hand and heavy enough to make it tremble. "My Lord!" She kissed it and before he could see it as clearly as he wanted to she put it back and tucked the bag between herself and the arm of the down-filled sofa.

"Your son," she said. "Will I see him?"

"Maybe not this trip. Certainly next fall if he comes to school."

"I've torn down the doll house," she said.

"You'd done that the last time I was here."

"It was rotting. And they claimed it was on the right of way when they started to widen October Lane."

For a long while they sat drinking their tea and sherry, each in his own world, listening to the great old clock in the hall. Off in the distance someone was using a chain saw. "Old people cut down trees," she said. "They can't get enough light or they're afraid a limb will fall on the roof and crush them. Or they discover how expensive it is to have leaves raked."

Oakley, if he came to school here, could keep her yard raked. "Or how expensive firewood is." He leaned forward, took a biscuit from a tin.

"That too," she said. "They've been sawing on it two days. Katie Darleen sent me those biscuits."

The minute he bit into it he knew why he had always thought her tea was good. The crackers were so stale anything would taste fresh afterward. He poured himself a sherry and filled her almost empty glass.

When she'd finished her glass and poured herself a third she placed it before her and regarded it with pleasure. "That will be all. Two." Then she asked what he knew she would. Something personal, something really none of her business but as if it were the most natural thing in the world to pry. "You're still separated?"

"Divorced."

"Oh, that bad."

"Worse. I had to take Oakley from her."

"Now that I don't believe in. Except in dire cases."

To keep from wasting time he would tell her the truth: his wife had brought in a man half her age, ten years older than Oakley. Oakley's Mountain Patrol Leader, as a matter of fact. Why be evasive? All of his friends in Virginia had known before he had.

"A person half her age. Sounds more like male menopause." Shardey was drinking the sherry with great appreciation, looking into it, through it, pausing, sipping. "Poor girl. Some women find it impossible to act their age. Especially at that time of life. And the Patrol Leader? Looking for a mother of course. Since he can't sleep with his own."

"He'd been married and destroyed his own daughter." Shardey nodded as if she knew the Patrol Leader perfectly.

"I had to take Oakley away. He twisted Oakley's neck in a fight."

"A play fight?"

"Oakley was trying to drive him away."

Shardey shook her head sadly.

"The neurosurgeon says there's absolutely nothing wrong with his neck but Oakley still stands with his head down and bent. He can hold his head up but he won't. Sometimes I think it's to aggravate me, to punish me for taking him away. That was over three years ago."

"No. That won't do. Not at all. Not at all." She set the sherry down and wiped her mouth with the back of her hand, then considered her palm, her life-line, as if there she would find what she wanted to say to him. He remembered how thoroughly she could project concentration and he knew whatever she said now she would mean with all her heart. "Maybe if you would forgive his mother, he could forgive you." She shook her head: the last sherry had been a mistake. "He needs someone to show him what forgiveness is." She pushed the bottle and the tumbler away from her end of the tray and said: "I'd heard all that at the time of the separation. I just didn't know whether to believe it." She looked at him closely. "And you?"

"I'm marking time."

"There's no such thing," she said sternly, "you go backward or you go forward."

"I stand still," he smiled, hoping to lure her out of her serious, prying mood.

"So does anybody who can't forgive the past."

"You mean 'forget'."

"I mean 'forgive'. You can't forget until you forgive."

A cloud passing or the shrubs moving at the window, something was shifting the light in the room. In the distance the tree fell, and some men were hollering and a dog barking. He glanced at his watch. He'd been here an hour. Longer than he'd meant to stay. Oakley would be back at the Inn soon. "This man who's coming. I'm afraid I'm not going to be able to wait."

"He'll be here. You just wait. I'm proud of him because I saved him from withdrawing completely from this world."

He would humor her awhile longer then get back up the hill before sunset. "Why do you think we should meet?"

"He's somebody. Like you. You're somebody. Thanks to me, both of you. He had intelligence but no courage. I hope he never knows: I'm the one who gave him courage. I made him do things he didn't want to do. I knew enough about stage fright to know how to bring him out. He had looks, talent. . . . Photography!" She remembered with triumph.

And in triumph she lifted the wig straight off her head. She held it aloft as if she had never seen it before, as if it were something dead she threw it to the other end of the sofa. "Photography! He'd taken pictures in the war. Then when I got him to pose nude for the art classes he got interested in bodies. Nudes."

He didn't know how to stop her. She was talking about him. He, himself, was the one who had posed. Drinking his sherry as if it were water he studied the tea table to keep from grinning and from staring at her almost bald head with its halo of white baby hair. Something was caught on top of her head, he did not want to see exactly what; but he knew he could not keep from glancing at it soon. "That was me, Shardey," he said soberly. "I'm the one who took pictures. . . ."

"No no no. You teach. He did a marvelous book of nudes. I've got it here. I'll show it to you. Then fashion magazines started sending him to Rome and Paris and then. . . ."

"That was me, Shardey."

"No no. You teach." She was insistent, threatened by the possibility of such a mistake.

"That's right. I teach photography. In the Art Department. In Virginia. You remember I came back here between assignments to teach one semester and stayed three years." Had she forgotten that he had married here, had Oakley here and that she had warned him the marriage would be the end of his career as an artist? And had not come to the wedding.

When she looked down he could stare at the thing caught on top of her head. At first he thought it was a ribbon tied to a lock of hair, but then he saw it was a gold ready-made bow, not tied on but one from a package stuck deliberately on the crown of her head, like a star on a tilted Christmas tree.

She grinned her strong square grin as if she knew how

foolish she looked, but then her face became fretful. "Where is it?" she asked, feeling about her on the sofa and under the cushions.

"There." He pointed to the wig where she had thrown it.

She stared at it trying to make it out. "Not that dead cat," she said. "My Lord." He did not understand. "My crucifix."

"In your bag," he pointed to her side.

Again she fumbled deep down between the sofa arm and springs and fished up the leather bag. She seemed to forget he was there as she pulled the drawstrings open. She turned the bag upside down and the gold Christ fell out heavily into her lap. The crucifix seemed even larger and brighter now in the slanting light and he wanted her to hold it up for him to see. It was ornate enough to be Byzantine and heavy enough to make him think she would drop it.

"Aren't you afraid someone will take it?" He asked as she rolled it back up in the old bag.

"Anybody can have it who wants it. That's how I got it. I simply asked."

Knowing her blunt and direct ways he could believe her. But now she was again in her own reverie, placing it carefully back in the bag and plunging the bag down by the arm of the sofa. "I could not have lived my life otherwise," she said. "When there is no future there's only faith."

She looked, sitting there grinning, with the halo of hair

and the fool bow, completely mad and like no one he had ever known. If she would put the wig back on, he would know what to say to her. "All right, then," he held out his hand.

"What?" she asked.

"Your bag. Give it to me."

"Too late. You've already asked all the wrong questions." She quit grinning, became mock serious, placed her palm on her scalp. "My head is getting cold." She glanced at the wig without seeming to recognize it, then retrieved it and pulled it down over each ear as if it were a stocking cap. "Now you see it. Now you don't." The sherry was making him drowsy and the room seemed, as often was the case around Shardey, like a stage.

Maybe now would be the time to begin telling her how she still gave him courage but she did not seem to be aware of him. Gradually her eyes were closing and now gradually her head was falling forward and once or twice her fingers fluttered and her thumbs were turning into the cradle of her palms. In the paling light he could not see if she were breathing or not, but soon she began snoring in great healthy exhalations.

He studied her intently so he could remember her whenever he needed to, slumped sideways in a peaceful sleep. A plain old Irish woman with a white moustache who seemed at the moment almost like a part of himself. He wanted to tiptoe out and not blur the picture but he knew he shouldn't. "Wake up, good soul," he thought. He studied his watch and knew Oakley was waiting for him. When he looked back up she was watching him with her piercing gaze, her encompassing smile.

"Shardey . . ." he began.

"Time!" she said, "Yes, it's time."

As he hugged her he knew that she knew it was probably for the last time. She would, though, have none of soft sentiment. "Off you go," she said and slapped his back.

On the way up the hill he sat on the rock wall to shake gravel from his Weejuns. While he sat there he could hear from far off someone singing "Lucy in the Sky with Diamonds." The music was coming from over the hill: the Chi Phis or Betas celebrating spring and open windows, not with punk rock, but with a medley of Beatles songs.

He continued to sit on the wall even though people passing in cars were looking at him sitting there. He had no inclination to stand up and move on. He wondered what would happen if he just stayed there until dark or until someone came and got him.

As he sat there he remembered a funny thing. In the mornings in the doll house he would be stretching and saying "Ho ho ho!" and hitting the wooden ceiling with his hands and taking up half the floor when he sat on the little rug to put on his shoes and look out the window. He was the biggest thing in the world. And then as he walked up this hill he would get smaller and smaller and smaller until he was smaller than anyone by the time he got to campus and his class.

Then late in the afternoon walking down this same walk he would grow larger and larger and when he stretched himself out on the brass bed he was again enormous and dreamed huge dreams. Now his life seemed that way to him. He had grown larger and larger until his marriage and then afterward smaller and smaller until now he sat with his feet hardly touching the gravel. Marking time. Which Shardey said was impossible. But what if he stopped living in the past? He stood, straightened stiffly and groaned a bit.

At first he walked slowly wondering what would happen if he forgave her as Shardey had said. It didn't seem likely anytime soon. But just to suppose: for one thing he might not have to pay Oakley's huge therapy bills. That alone made it worth considering. He was walking faster now and pretending as he stepped out in long strides that he was growing larger and larger and larger. By the time he got to the hospital at the top of the hill the Inn was only one giant-step away. And if Oakley were on the lawn or in one of the wicker chairs on the porch, he would bend over and with just the tip of his finger and his thumb he would pick Oakley up by his head and hold him up as high as a telephone pole and looking down at him say in a voice louder than a sonic boom, so loud not many people would be able to hear: "We're going to learn about forgiveness, you sonovabitch."

The Cat and the Coffee Drinkers

I SOMETIMES wonder if the generation of mothers who from 1910 to 1940 sent their five-year-olds to the kindergarten of Miss Effie Barr had much of an idea what their children were learning in her one-room schoolhouse. Even though in 1930 the Southern town in which she lived was no longer small, and even though she was already in her seventies, Miss Effie knew all of the children in her school a year, and often longer, before they appeared before her for lessons. My mother, properly gloved and chapeaued, began taking me to call on her when I was four.

Her house was a good place to visit. It was large and grey, and was set well back from the same street that I lived on. It was the last "white" house before the Negro part of town, and the first Negro houses had been, up until the Depression, part of the Barr properties. There were mossy brick steps leading from a hitching post up to a gravel walk that curved between overgrown boxwoods to a low porch with twelve slender columns. There, in the summer, in the shade of water oaks, Miss Effie, dressed in black, would be sitting, knitting or embroidering, while her big grey cat sat at, and sometimes on, her feet. Slow, uncertain music would be coming through open windows from the music room, where her older sister, Miss Hattie, gave piano lessons.

Miss Effie never seemed to watch a child on such visits, or offer him anything like cookies or lemonade, or say anything to endear herself to a youngster. Instead, she would talk lady talk with the mother and, hardly pausing, say to the child, "You can pull up the wild onions on the lawn if you've nothing better to do." There was no suggestion in her voice that it was a game or that there would be a reward. She simply stated what could be done if one took a notion. Usually a child did.

There was no nonsense about Miss Effie. One morning in late September, my mother and I were standing with eleven other mothers and children on the porch. Miss Effie looked everyone over carefully from where she stood with one hand on the screen door. She checked a list in the other hand against the young faces on the porch, to be sure that these were the children she had chosen from the forty or more who had visited her in the summer. Apparently satisfied, or at least reconciled to another year of supplementing her income (for no Southern lady of her generation "worked"), she opened the door wide and said, in her indifferent tone, "Children inside." When one mother tried to lead her reluctant son into the dark parlor, Miss Effie said, "Mothers outside."

When the children were all inside and the mothers outside, Miss Effie latched the screen, thanked the mothers for bringing the children, and reminded them that classes began at eight-thirty and ended at noon. The tuition, two dollars a week, would be acceptable each Friday, and each child, as part of his training, should be given the responsibility of delivering the money in an envelope bearing the parent's signature. She thanked the mothers again in such a way that there was nothing for them to do except wander together in a group down the gravel walk.

Miss Effie then turned to us, who were standing somewhat closer together than was necessary, in the center of the dark parlor, and said, "Since this is your first day, I want to show you everything. Then you won't be wondering about things while you should be listening."

She made us look at the Oriental carpet, the grandfather clock, the bookcases of leatherbound volumes, the shelves on which were collections of rocks, shells, birds' nests, and petrified wood. She offered to let us touch, just this once, any of these things.

She would not let us into the music room, which was then empty, but indicated through the doorway the imported grand piano, the red plush seat where Miss Hattie sat during lessons, the music racks, the ferns, and the window seats, which she said were full of sheet music.

"You're never to go in there," she said. "I don't go in there myself."

Next, she showed us the dining room, the den, and the hallway, and at the foot of the stairs she said, "We're going upstairs, and then you'll never go up there again." Barbara Ware, one of three girls in our class, began to whimper. "Don't worry," Miss Effie said, "you'll come back down. But there'll be no reason to go up again. I want you to see everything, so you won't have to ask personal questions, which would certainly be the height of impoliteness, wouldn't it? I mean, if you started wanting to know, without my telling you, where I sleep and which window is Miss Hattie's, I'd think you were rude, wouldn't I? I'll show you everything, so you won't be tempted to ask personal questions."

We went upstairs, and she showed us her room and where she kept her shoes (in the steps leading up to the side of her four-poster bed), where she hung her clothes (in two large armoires) and kept her hatbox (in a teakwood sea chest). The cat, she said, slept on the sea chest if he happened to be home at night.

She then knocked on the door of Miss Hattie's room and asked her sister, who was inside, if we might look in. Miss Hattie agreed to a short visit. After that, Miss Effie showed us the upstairs bathroom and explained that the bathtub faucet dripped all night and that was why a towel was kept under it.

Downstairs again, Miss Effie let us see the "new" kitchen, which was built in 1900, and the back porch, which had been screened in only four years before, and which had a small door through which the cat could come and go as he liked. We were as fascinated by everything as we would have been if we had never seen a house before.

"Now, out the back door. All of you." She made us all stand on the ground, off the steps, while she lowered herself, step by step, with the aid of a cane that she kept on a nail by the door. "Now you've seen my house and you won't see it again. Unless I give your mothers fruitcake and coffee at Christmas. And I don't think I will. Not this year. Do you ever get tired of fruitcake and coffee at Christmas?"

We said we did, since it was clear that she did.

"Over there is the barn, and we'll see it some other time, and that is the greenhouse, and we'll be seeing it often. And here is the classroom, where we'll be." She pointed with her cane to a square brick building that before the Civil War had been the kitchen. The door was open.

She shepherded us along a brick walk with her cane, not allowing any of us near enough to her to topple her over. At the door, she said, "Go on in."

We crowded in, and when we were all through the door she summoned us back out. "Now, which of you are boys?" The nine boys raised their hands, following her lead. "And which girls?" The three girls had already separated themselves from the boys, and nodded together. "All right, then, young gentlemen," she said, regarding us, "let's let the young ladies enter first. Or I may think you're all young ladies."

The girls, looking timid and pleased, entered. We started in after them.

"Wait just a minute, young gentlemen," she said. "Haven't you forgotten something?" We looked about for another girl.

"Me!" she announced. "You've forgotten me!" She passed through our huddle, separating us with her stick, and marched into the kitchen.

Inside, as well as out, the kitchen was mainly of brick. The walls and floor were brick, and the hearth and the huge chimney, except for a closet-cupboard on each side of it, were brick. The ceiling, however, was of beams and broad boards, and the windows were of wavy glass in casements that opened out like shutters. There were three large wooden tables, and at each table four chairs.

Again she had to show us everything. The fireplace would be used in only the coldest weather, she said. At other times, an iron stove at one side of the room would be used. A captain's chair, between the fireplace and the stove, was her own and not to be touched by us. A sewing table, overflowing with yarn and knitting needles, was for her own use, and not for ours. One cupboard, the one near her, held dishes. She opened its door. She would let us see in the other cupboard later. The tables and chairs and, at the far end of the room, some pegs for coats were all ours, to do with as we pleased. It was, she explained, our schoolroom, and therefore, since we were young ladies and gentlemen, she was sure we would keep it clean.

As a matter of fact, she saw no reason why we should not begin with the first lesson: Sweeping and Dusting. She opened the other cupboard and showed us a mop, a bucket, some rags and brushes, and three brooms. We were not divided into teams; we were not given certain areas to see who could sweep his area cleanest; we were simply told that young ladies should naturally be able to sweep and that young gentlemen at some times in their lives would certainly be expected to sweep a room clean.

The instruction was simple: "You get a good grip on the handle and set to." She handed out the three brooms and started us boys sweeping from the fireplace toward the front door. She made simple corrections: "You'll raise a dust, flirting the broom upward. Keep it near the floor." "Hold lower on the handle. You'll get more dirt." "Don't bend over. You'll be tired before the floor is clean."

When we swept, Miss Effie made a big red enamel coffeepot of coffee on a small alcohol stove. Since the room had not been swept, she admitted, all summer, there was a respectable pile of brick dust, sand, and sweepings near the door by the time she said, "We'll have lunch now." It was already ten o'clock. "After lunch, I'll teach you how to take up trash and to dust. Everyone needs to know that."

"Lunch," it happened, was half a mug of coffee each. One spoon of sugar, she said, was sufficient if we felt it necessary to use sugar at all (she didn't); there was milk for those who could not or would not (she spoke as though using milk were a defect of character) take their coffee black. I daresay not any of us had ever had coffee before, and Robert Barnes said he hadn't.

"Good!" Miss Effie said. "So you have learned something today."

Miriam Wells, however, said, on reflection, that her parents wouldn't approve of her drinking coffee.

"Very well," Miss Effie said. "Don't drink it. And the next time I offer you any, if I ever do, simply say 'No, thank you, Ma'am.'" (The next day, Miriam Wells was drinking it along with the rest of us.) "Let's get this clear right this minute— your parents don't need to know what you do when you're under my instruction."

Her firm words gave us a warm feeling, and from that moment on the schoolroom became a special, safe, and rather secret place.

That day, we learned, further, how to rinse out mugs and place them in a pan to be boiled later, how to take up trash, and how to dust. At noon, we were taught the right way to put on our sweaters or coats, how to approach, one at a time, our teacher (or any lady we should happen to be visiting) and say "Thank you" (for the coffee or whatever we had been served), and how to say goodbye and turn and leave the room without running or laughing. It wasn't as easy as you may think.

THE NEXT morning, Robert Barnes was waiting on his steps when I walked by his house. Since he and I lived nearer to the Barrs' than any of the other children, we were the first to arrive at the schoolhouse.

Miss Effie sat in her captain's chair brushing the cat, which lay on a tall stool in front of her. We entered without speaking. Without looking up, Miss Effie said, "Now, young gentlemen, let's try that again—outside. Take off your caps before you step through the door, and say 'Good morning, Ma'am' as you come through the door. Smile if you feel like it. Don't if you don't." She herself did not smile as we went out and reentered in the manner she suggested. However, this time she looked directly at us when she returned our good mornings. Later, each child who entered the room in what she felt to be a rude way was sent out to try again.

Strangely enough, she did not smile at anyone, and looking back I see now that part of her efficiency was that she treated each child as an adult and each lesson as though it were a serious task. Even though there were occasional crying scenes or temper tantrums among us, she herself never lost her firm, rational approach. Sitting in her captain's chair, dressed in black from neck to toe, except for a cameo, small gold loop earrings, and a gold opal ring on her right hand, she was usually as solemn and considerate as a judge on his bench. It is strange that I can remember her calm expression and the dignity of her bearing, but not one feature of her angular face.

That morning, Miss Effie waited until all of us were properly in before addressing us as a class. "This is Mr. Thomas," she said of the cat on the stool. "He's a no-good cat and he doesn't like children, so leave him alone. I'd have nothing to do with him myself except that he happens to belong to me because his mother and grandmother belonged to me. They were no good, either. But since he does belong to me and since he is here, we may as well talk about cats."

She showed us how to brush a cat, how he liked to be rubbed under his neck, how he didn't like his ears or whiskers touched, how his ears turned to pick up sounds, how he stretched and shut his paw pads when he was tickled on the stomach or feet, and how he twitched his tail when annoyed. "Mr. Thomas is a fighter," she said, and let us look at the scars from a dozen or more fights, "and he's getting too old to fight, but he hasn't got sense enough to know that."

She looked at us where we stood in more or less a large circle around her. "Now, let's see, I don't know your names. I know your mothers, but not your names." She would, she said, indicate us one at a time and we were to give our names in clear, loud voices while looking her right in the eye. Then we were to choose a chair at one of the three tables. "I hate the way most people become shy when they say their names. Be proud of it and speak up."

When the young ladies had finished giving their names, she said they did admirably well; they chose to sit at the same table. One or two boys shouted their names in a silly fashion and had to repeat. One or two looked away, to decide on a chair or to watch the cat, they claimed, and so had to repeat. I did not speak loud enough and had to say my name three times. One lad refused to say his name a second time, and that day and the next she called him Mr. No-Name. The third day afterward, he did not appear, nor the fourth nor fifth, and the next week a new boy from the waiting list gave his name in a perfect fashion and took Mr. No-Name's place.

We learned about cats and names the second day, then.

202 THE HAT OF MY MOTHER

The following day, Barbara Ware and Robert Barnes distinguished themselves by claiming to like their coffee black with no sugar, just the way Miss Effie was convinced it should be drunk.

At the end of the second week, we reviewed what we had learned by sweeping and dusting the room again. And each day we practiced coming in and leaving properly and saying our name in a way that sounded as though we were proud of it and of ourselves—which by then we were.

The third week, putting down the cat brush and shooing Mr. Thomas off the stool, Miss Effie said that she, too, was proud of the way we identified ourselves with eyes level and unblinking. "But now," she said, "I want to teach you to give a name that is not your own. Without any shiftiness."

She sat with both thin hands clasping the arms of her chair and gave a short lecture. Not everyone, she said, was entitled to know your name. Some people of a certain sort would ask when it was none of their business. It would be unnecessarily rude to tell them so. But we could simply tell such people a name that had nothing whatever to do with our own. She did not mention kidnappings, but talked rather about ruthless salesmen, strangers on buses and trains, and tramps and beggars wandering through the neighborhood.

For the purpose of practice, all of the young ladies would

learn to give, in a courteous, convincing manner, the name "Polly Livingstone." The boys would be, when asked, "William Johnson" (a name I can still give with much more conviction than my own). That day and the next, each of us gave his real name before the coffee break, and after coffee his false name. We liked the exercises wherein we went up to her, shook her hand if she offered it, and gave our false names, confronting, without staring, her solemn gaze with ours. If we smiled, or twisted, we had to stand by the fireplace until we could display more poise.

AT THE end of the first month, Miss Effie said that she was fairly well pleased with our progress. "I have taught you, thus far, mainly about rooms. Most people spend most of their lives in rooms, and now you know about them." She mentioned some of the things we had learned. "What else have we learned about rooms?" she then asked, letting Mr. Thomas out the window onto the sunny ledge where he liked to sit.

"How to drink coffee," Miriam Wells said, rather proudly.

"No," Miss Effie said, "that has to do with another series, which includes how to accept things and how to get rid of things you don't want—fat meat, bones, seeds, pits, peelings, and (she added under her breath) parents." She paused for a moment and looked pleased, as though she might wink or smile, but her angular face did not change its expression very much. "No. Besides, I'm not pleased with the way you're drinking coffee." She then said for the first time a speech that she repeated so often that by the end of the year we sometimes shouted it in our play on the way home. "Coffee is a beverage to be enjoyed for its flavor. It is not a food to be enriched with milk and sugar. Only certain types of people try to gain nourishment from it. In general, they are the ones, I suspect, who show their emotions in public." (We had, I'm sure, no idea what the speech meant.) She expected all of us by June, possibly by Christmas, to be drinking it black. "Is there anything else we need to know about rooms?" she asked.

"How to build them," Phillip Pike said.

"That," Miss Effie said, "you can't learn from me. Unfortunately. I wish I knew." She looked thoughtfully out the window to the ledge on which Mr. Thomas was grooming himself. "Windows!" she said. "How to clean windows."

Again the cupboard was opened, and by noon the next day we knew how to clean windows, inside and out, and how to adjust all the shades in a room to the same level.

When it turned cold in November, cold enough for the stove but not the fireplace, we settled down to the real work that gave Miss Effie's kindergarten its reputation. Reading. Miss Effie liked to read, and it was well known in the town and especially among the public-school teachers that the two or three hundred children she had taught had grown up reading everything they could find. She assured us that even though we were only five years old, we would be reading better than the third grade schoolchildren by the end of the year.

Each morning, the stove was already hot when we arrived. She would brush Thomas a while, and then, when we were all in our places and warm, she would hand out our reading books, which we opened every day to the first page and laid flat before us on the tables. While we looked at the first page, she began heating the big red enamel pot of coffee, and also, because we now needed nourishment to keep warm, a black iron pot of oatmeal. Then Miss Effie would sit down, allow Thomas to jump into her lap, and begin reading, always from the first page, in an excited tone. She would read to the point exactly where we had finished the day before, so that from necessity she read faster each day, while we turned our pages, which we knew by heart, when we saw her ready to turn hers.

Then, one after another, we went up to her and sat on Mr. Thomas's stool by the stove and read aloud to her while those at the tables either listened or read or played with architectural blocks. The child on the stool was rewarded at the end of each sentence with two spoonfuls of oatmeal if he read well, one if not so well. Since we each read twice, once before coffee and once after, we did not really get hungry before we left the school at noon. Of course, those who read fast and well ate more oatmeal than the others.

In addition to the reading lessons, which were the most important part of the day, we learned to take money and shopping lists to Mr. Zenacher's grocery store, to pay for groceries, and to bring them back with the change. Usually two or three of us went together to the store, which was in the next block. At the same time, three or four others might be learning to paint flowerpots or to catch frying-size chickens in the chicken yard back of the barn.

On sunny days that winter, we would all go out to the greenhouse for an hour and learn to reset ferns and to start bulbs on wet beds of rock. In March, we learned how to rake Miss Effie's tennis court, to fill in any holes with powdery sand, and to line up and tie strings properly so that later a Negro yardman could mark the lines on the court with lime. The tennis court was for rent to high school girls and boys in the afternoons during the spring and summer.

By Easter time, we were all proficient sweepers, dusters, shoppers, bulb-setters, readers, and black-coffee drinkers. Miss Effie herself, now that spring was in the air, hated to sit all morning by the stove, where we'd been all winter. Usually, after an hour or so of reading, all aloud and at once, we would follow her into the yard and prune the "first-breath-of-spring," the jessamine, the yellow bells, and the peach and pear trees. We kept the branches we cut off and we stuck them in buckets of water in the greenhouse. Miss Effie printed a sign that said "Flowers for Sale," and we helped her tie it to a tree near the sidewalk. In addition to the flowering branches that we had forced, she sold ferns and the jonquils that we had set and that were now in bud.

ALL IN all, spring was a busy time. And I remember only one other thing we learned. One warm May morning, we arrived to find Mr. Thomas, badly torn about the ears, his eyes shut, his breathing noisy, on a folded piece of carpet near the open door of the schoolhouse. We wanted to pet him and talk to him, but Miss Effie, regarding him constantly, said no, that he had obviously been not only a bad cat but a foolish one. She believed he had been hit by a car while running from some dogs, and that that was how the dogs got to him. (She and Miss Hattie had heard the fight during the night.) At any rate, he had managed to crawl under the steps, where the dogs couldn't get to him any more. At dawn she had come down and thrown hot water on the dogs and rescued him.

As soon as a Negro boy from her cousin's office arrived (her cousin was a doctor), she was going to teach us how to put a cat to sleep, she said.

We pointed out that he already seemed to be asleep.

"But," she explained, not taking her eyes from the cat, "we are going to put him to sleep so that he won't wake up."

"You're going to kill him?" Robert Barnes said.

"You could say that."

We were all greatly disturbed when we understood that this was the last we would see of Mr. Thomas. But Miss Effie had no sympathy, apparently, for the cat or for us. "He is suffering, and even if he is a no-good cat, he shouldn't suffer." When Barbara Ware began to whimper, Miss Effie said, "Animals are not people." Her tone was severe enough to stop Barbara from crying.

After the Negro boy had arrived with the package and left, Miss Effie stopped her reading, and, going to one of the cupboards, she got out a canvas bag with a drawstring top. "Now, if you young ladies will follow us, I'll ask the young gentlemen to bring Mr. Thomas."

We all rushed to be the ones to lift the piece of carpet and bear Mr. Thomas after her, through her garden, to the tool shed.

"Just wrap the carpet around him. Tight. Head and all," she instructed when we reached the tool shed.

After we had him wrapped securely, Miss Effie opened the package and read the label: "Chloroform." She explained to us the properties of the chemical while we rolled the cat tighter and stuck him, tail first, into the canvas bag. Miss Effie asked us to stand back and hold our breath. She then soaked a large rag with the liquid and poured the rest directly onto the cat's head and on the carpet. She poked the rag into the rolled carpet so that it hid Mr. Thomas completely. She then drew the drawstring tight and slung the cat, bag and all, into the tool shed. She shut the door firmly and latched it. "That'll cut out the air," she said.

Back in the schoolhouse, we tried to listen as she read, without her usual excited tone, but we were all thinking about Mr. Thomas in the tool shed.

"Well," she finally said, "if you will excuse me a moment, I'll go see if my cat is dead."

We watched from the windows as she walked with her cane through the garden to the tool shed. We could see her open the door and bend over the sack for a long time. At last, she straightened up and locked the door again. She came back with the same unhalting gait and stood for a moment in the sun before the open door of the schoolhouse.

"When I dismiss you, you're to go straight home. And if they want to know why you're home early"—she stopped and studied the ground as though she had lost there her cameo or her words—"tell them the only thing Miss Effie had to teach you today was how to kill a cat."

Without waiting for us to leave, she walked in her usual

dignified fashion down the brick walk and up the back steps and into her house, shutting the kitchen door firmly behind her. I know that that was not the last day of school, for I remember helping to spread tablecloths over the reading tables, and I remember helping to serve teacakes to the mothers who came the last day and stood on the tennis court near a table where Miss Hattie was serving coffee. But the final, definite picture I have of Miss Effie is that of her coming through the garden from the tool shed and standing in the doorway a moment to say that she had nothing more to teach us.

Ah Love! Ah Me!

IT HAPPENED six years ago when I was in my third year of high school that I saw Sara Nell Workman for the first time and, not to be sentimental, I liked the girl. I liked her so much, in fact, that I would go to the library and read the cards in the back of the books to find the ones she had borrowed. I would take these out and read them carefully, including one called *Needlepoint and Needlecraft.*

"It's for my sister," I said hoarsely to the librarian, who was looking at me curiously. There were some penciled notes in the margin about hemstitching, and whether Sara made these notes or not, I don't know. (At the time I liked to imagine that she did, and I read them over and over: "Two skeins of black, two orange, one yellow, and the tulip stencil. Mother's Day, 17 Days.")

But when you're sixteen, you can't keep reading marginal notes over and over. At least I couldn't. And so the time came when I decided to ask Sara for a date. That day at school I couldn't find her by herself, and juniors in high school don't just up and ask a girl for a date in front of everybody.

At home that night I went out into the hall where the

phone was and shut the door behind me. I wrote Sara's number on the pad and then one sentence: "Sara—*Jezebel* is on Friday night and I was just wondering if you'd like to see it with me."

That sounded casual and easy enough to say, but when I heard the phone ringing the number, I got excited and crumpled the paper in my hand. For a second I considered hanging up, but then someone said, "Hello."

"Oh," I said. "May I speak to Sara Workman?"

"This is she," she said, rather impatiently it seemed.

"Oh, Sara," I said, "uh, this is Dave. . . ."

"Yes," she said.

"Do you know what our history assignment is for tomorrow?" I asked hopelessly.

"Just a minute," she said. She got her book and gave me the assignment. I thanked her and hung up. Then I untwisted the phone wire and went back to my room to brood.

About an hour later I decided that the thing to do was to jump up suddenly without thinking, rush into the hall, and phone her before I had a chance to become flustered. I jumped up quickly, but then I turned back to the dresser and brushed my hair before rushing out of the room.

When Sara answered the phone, I blurted out, "Would you like to go to the show with me Friday night? This is Dave."

"Well, I don't know," Sara said very slowly and coolly. "What's on?"

"I don't know," I said. "I thought maybe we'd just go mess around uptown."

"What?" she asked.

"I mean I don't know," I said. "*Lucy Belle* or something like that." I really couldn't remember.

"*Jezebel!*" she said. "Bette Davis. Yeah! I'd love to see it."

"Okay," I said. "Good-bye."

The next day I avoided meeting Sara alone. In the line at the cafeteria she leaned around two people and said to me, "That was you last night, wasn't it?"

"Yeah," I said.

She smiled, and for a moment I was afraid that she was going to laugh, but she didn't.

Friday night at eight o'clock when we were leaving Sara's house, Mr. Workman, who looked like John L. Lewis, asked, "Who's driving?"

"I am," I said.

"You got a license?"

"Yes, sir."

"Well," he hollered, as we went down the walk, "just see to it that you get Sara back here safe. And before eleven o'clock."

"Yes, sir," I said.

"Eleven o'clock, Sara," he screamed.

She was embarrassed, but she hollered back, "Yes, sir."

At the theater we had to stand in line, and when finally we did get seats they were in the third row. My neck was hurting before the newsreel was over, but Sara didn't seem to mind looking straight up at the screen.

When the picture was almost over, she caught me looking at her. "Whatsa matter?" she whispered.

"Headache," I said. "I think it's from looking straight. . . ."

"Shhhh . . ." she whispered. On the screen Bette Davis was risking death by yellow fever to be with her man and nurse him.

Sara was very quiet when we came out of the show. As we walked down Main Street, I said, "Do you think she should have stayed with him? She probably caught yellow fever, too."

"It's not a matter of what you should or shouldn't do," Sara said. "For when you love a man, nothing can tear you away."

"Good gosh!" I said. Above us a neon light flickered off and on and buzzed as though it would explode.

We stood in front of Shaeffer's drugstore for a minute. It was ten-fifteen then, and Sara was worried about getting home.

"Just something to drink," she said; "we haven't time to eat."

She ordered a chocolate milkshake, and I wanted one, too, but I thought it would look kind of sophisticated to order something for my headache. I couldn't remember ammonia and Coke, and so I asked the waiter what he had for a headache.

"Aspirin, epsom salts, litho-bromide, anything you want," he said.

"Bring me a litho-bromide," I said, trying to sound weary, "and a Coke."

"Still hurts?" Sara asked softly.

I smiled at her without answering.

John Bowerman and two other seniors came in and took the booth next to ours. All of the booths and tables were filling with the crowd from the movie.

The waiter brought the order. My Coke was in one glass, two litho-bromide tablets were in the bottom of an empty glass, and there was a big glass of water.

I'd never taken a litho-bromide, and I didn't know that the tablets were supposed to be dropped into a glass of water where they would fizz while dissolving. I just shook the tablets out into my hand, popped them in my mouth, and swallowed them one at a time as though they were aspirin. Then I drank half the Coke while Sara tasted her milkshake.

I drank the rest of the Coke and tried to pretend that nothing was happening. Sara put down her glass and stared at me, terrified. I sounded like somebody gargling under a barrel.

"It always does this," I said bravely. But by then the rumblings from the mixture were too ominous to be ignored by me or the people in the other booths. Everyone was staring at my stomach.

"Everybody's looking at you," Sara whispered. She was so red that I was afraid she was going to cry.

"Sounds like somebody churning buttermilk," John Bowerman said, coming around to our booth.

"He's effervescing!" the waiter announced happily to the astonished customers. "Just listen to his fizz!"

"Sara," I said, and I was going to tell her to get out of there, but I was afraid to open my mouth to say anything else. The rumbling just sounded deeper when I did, like drumming on a hollow log.

"Doc Shaeffer!" John Bowerman called out when Sara told him what I had done.

Doc Shaeffer climbed over the prescription counter. "Stand back!" he ordered the crowd that was gathering around our booth. They stepped back as though they expected me to explode.

"It's nothing serious," Doc Shaeffer said. "Get his head lower than his stomach. Give me a hand with him."

"He says it always does this," Sara said.

"That's pretty hard to believe," Doc motioned to John Bowerman and the two seniors picked me up and carried me to the prescription counter. They stretched me out and let my head hang off with my mouth open. A dogfight couldn't have attracted more attention. Doc Shaeffer brought a wet towel from the back of the drugstore. Sara stood beside me and rubbed my forehead with it.

"Sara," I said, and I suppose now I must have sounded rather melodramatic to the other people, "you won't leave me, will you?"

"Oh, my goodness!" Sara said. "What time is it?"

"Ten till eleven," John Bowerman glanced at his watch.

Sara dropped the wet towel in my face. "I've got to be home by eleven!"

"I'll take you," John said.

I took the towel off my face in time to see them stopping by the booth for Sara's pocketbook. She didn't even look back at me.

The four or five people who were standing by me went back to their tables. I lay quietly on the counter and watched the light above swaying gently in the noisy room.

Gradually, two by two, the people left, and the noise of the dishes being stacked grew quieter and quieter. I watched the waiter turn the chairs upside down on the tables and felt sorry for him and for myself and for the whole pitiful world.

The Silent Scream

MY BIG toe hurts. Furthermore, it has been hurting. But because the pain did not commence suddenly—acute and intense as it is now—I do not know when it began. All I can say is: I do not remember when it was not there.

Of course I know, full well as you, that it is not without meaning and cause and purpose. But still it hurts.

"Well, man," you say, "get yourself off to a doctor."

"What for?" I ask. You know he'll shake hands and then wash his, and say: "Let's take a look at it."

He'll put a light on his forehead and squint through the bottom half of his bifocals and spread the toes and examine the nail. "I don't see anything," he says. "Except a little athlete's foot. Not as bad as mine." He washes his hands again.

I refrain from telling him that even with no scientific training I had made the same observations and that I was not paying to learn the condition of his feet. How bored I am with paying doctors to tell me how tired they are and how their backs ache! To hell with homey, bedsidey manners when my big toe aches fit to kill.

"Does it hurt when I do this?" He mashes it on each side. With effort I do not yell.

"Sir, it hurts all of the time and is especially sensitive to pressure."

He deliberately mashes as hard as he can from top to bottom. "And this?"

I do not kick him a good swift one under the chin.

He washes his hands. "Take off your shirt." "Undershirt." "Trousers." He finally gets to the point. "Strip." He wraps a tube around my arm. He listens to my lungs, my heart, through the stethoscope, then with his warm ear, thumping here and there and having me breathe deeply and not at all while he thumps away. He washes his hands.

"Stand on that foot." "Turn around." "Now on the other." "Hold still." "Now cough." "Spread your cheeks." "Say Ah." He washes his hands.

Then a family history. "All dead." "All of old age." He calculates: "But your father was only 36." I insist: "Old age." He seems not to understand what living with my mother could be like. No, no feet trouble in the entire family. Toes all fine and beautiful, even as far away as grandparents and second cousins.

Then my sex life. "Do I this?" And "Did I that?" "And at what age this and that?" "Everything at every age," I claim. All the time my big toe is aching so I can hardly answer, knowing I have spent my money for nothing, that he will assume an intelligence beyond his training and say: "I'd like for you to see a psychiatrist. I'll give you his number and also a prescription for that touch of athlete's foot." He is washing his hands again.

"The same remedy you use?" I ask, but it is lost on him.

"Try cutting your toenails square." Which I've done all my life. "And get larger shoes."

I put back on my sandals, thank him, estimating, as I tie my tie, another fifty dollars shot to hell. At least he hasn't referred me to a dentist. It'll be interesting to see whether it's the meek doctors or the meek dentists who end up owning this earth.

"If it's not better next week," he says, going through the Pilate act again, "get in touch with my secretary."

"Does she understand about toes?" I foolishly ask before I realize he means for another appointment. Thus my hope always betrays itself.

"But he was right," you say, "you should see a psychiatrist." Each age has its own follies. The intelligent in Chaucer's day subscribed to Humours. Well, man must have faith. Those who belong to churches think everyone should go; those who belong to psychiatrists think everyone should go.

"No thank you, sir." If I want a religion I'll take it straight and have faith in an Unknown, rather than a Known with ten toes, more or less, the same as I.

But I toy with the idea and go to the public library and look under toes in all the bibliographies and indices in all the books dealing with psychology and psychiatry. In one I come across a reference that makes great good sense: "Hypochondria . . . as a paranoid symptom." I read the passage, several pages with a case history of fifteen pages. It is beautiful. It makes sense. I read it three times and understand it so clearly that I am amazed to discover that my toe is still hurting just as much as ever.

"Aha," you say, "you understand intellectually but not emotionally. Only with a psychiatrist can you experience that."

Then I should go and be met at the door by a solemn face and a tone which suggests that we should by all means bury the dead. He shakes hands and I'm relieved to see does not wash his. No, he hurries me to the couch as if I do not see the reason for the rush. Sitting back of me, out of sight, he quickly, expertly, and with practice, takes his foot out of his shoe and with his fingertips tests the temperature of the water in the tub under the couch. I settle into a nice comfortable free association—the only thing free in the whole packaged deal—while he, his toe hurting, truth known, as much as mine, rolls up the cuffs of his trousers.

Then he interrupts, showing what I consider magic insight when he asks: "Does it hurt more if it is only partly in the water and partly out?" I say, "Yes." And if I did not have to go on talking, if I could listen carefully enough, I could hear his own toe dive completely under before he says: "Ah! It feels better completely under water." He remembers it should be a question. "Doesn't it?" I am moved almost to tears by his wisdom, his understanding, the implications of a great and curative knowledge.

Then I am to learn it all. Throw the mass of material in, set the formula, turn the crank, and out it comes, all neat and like a million others: "Left toe—incest, homosexuality, perversions of every imaginable sort. Right toe—unresolved Oedipus complex, fear of intercourse with own or any other wife, castration by father, thus the pain."

"For the toe is the penis," he says. As if I didn't know my penis from my big toe, for God's sake!

I accept or refuse it all. More material, another formula, turn the crank, whirr whirr. "The toe is a symbol for you. You are afraid of your own aggressions, especially toward women. You are afraid to kick the world (your father). By keeping it submerged you seek to return to the warm womb." He swishes his foot almost audibly in the tub.

"And Thursday is my lucky day," I say.

"We can talk about that during the next twenty-five dollars," he says.

No thank you. I'll let it ache. Which it's bound to do anyway. With this difference: now when the time comes I can afford a wheelchair with as many gears as an Italian racing bike. And taxicabs. And if necessary, someone to help me in and out of elevators. But give one of those aching-toed spooks all my money and I'll be lucky to afford a crutch-tip, and a candy bar for the janitor's son who would fetch it from the drugstore.

All is not black and bitter with me, even when my toe aches the most. For in 1965, Gemini will be in my first house in opposition to Taurus in my sixth and that will be excellent for my feet for my sun is in Aries.

In addition, a friend in Italy has had a wax toe effigy made and has hung it for me at an altar where one hangs such things. I send him money for candles which he keeps burning beneath. (But not close enough beneath, he has explained in answer to my letter, to melt the toe.)

What choice have I but to be encouraged?

In the meantime I go on living each day out and getting through the nights when it hurts the most, as best I can without moaning and disturbing the neighbors.

If it were my heart or my eyes which were causing me these sleepless nights, how much sympathy I would be offered. Ladies from various circles would come and sit on my porch and walk me about a bit and read to me from inspirational books. "Sunbeams" would come twice a year with crayon-colored paper baskets and would sing their song under my window.

But who, honestly, look deep in your heart, has ever had sympathy for a big toe? I remember when even I, myself, would have laughed.

Didn't W. C. Fields have a bad toe in a movie and didn't everyone howl with glee when it got stepped on or he forgot and kicked someone? Or was it Jiggs in the funny paper with his occasional gout? Certainly the Captain in "Katzenjammer Kids." If I were younger I'd propose as a topic for a Master's thesis: "The Major Pedal Digit in Dramatic and Graphic Humor During the American Renaissance." Except that it's probably already been done by someone at Columbia.

So now I live my days thus: in the mornings when there is a strong morning light through the jalousies, I get out my flashlight and magnifying glass and examine my toe as carefully as a jeweler an opal, in the hopes of finding yet some flaw overlooked in an examination of the previous day. But then the women in the beauty parlor next door begin calling to each other and pointing without shame through the window at me where I sit fully and correctly dressed except for one bare foot (for one must, regardless, keep up appearances). Naturally I can not continue then to sit, foot on thigh, looking at the thing which refuses to give outward sign of the inner hell.

For awhile, I went out every afternoon and, as the saying goes, "mingled." But then I found myself thinking either that I, in all the world, was the only one with a big toe that hurt, and hating everyone else; or I thought that everyone was secretly nursing an aching toe and at such moments I loved them all to the point of embarrassing tears which threatened to become sobs. Then there was nothing to do but hail a cab and return as quickly as possible to my room, there to shut the opaque jalousies against the stares of the women with their metal skulls and coils of hair.

On occasion, in the evenings, I try to forget the pain by going to the movies. But there I can not always follow the stories, for wondering if the big toes of Gary Cooper and Alan Ladd and Hedy Lamarr all hurt, and if that is why they keep such straight faces. More recently I have admired them more than Bette Davis and Susan Hayward, Brando and Dean and Newman, who betray their pain in every move.

Mainly now, afternoons and evenings, I have been staying in writing letters. My wife has written a note in answer, on the bottom of a page by her lawyer (these days she can not belch or fart without legal advice) suggesting that when the property is settled, I should perhaps find a woman, this time a real homemaker, whose toe hurts worse than mine, so I can get my mind off myself by thinking about hers. As if that would work. Even my scant knowledge of mathematics and human beings tells me that one aching toe plus one aching toe does not add up to zero aching toes. No. One plus one, in this case, adds up to two at least, and to two or three if one is lazy or not careful.

No, the whole suggestion is a strictly feminine one and I'll have none of it. Poor women. They know the only thing they're good for is having babies. Thus the conspiracy. But my wife had hers so why doesn't she pipe down? Why the campaign?

Well, it's too late now, far too late, to get worked up over a comment from a woman who kept me angry for fifteen years.

Nor can I join with those who try to persuade me that my suffering is economic in origin and cure. If for one moment I really believed that a working-class laborer's toe could hurt more than mine, I might be tempted to lose myself and my pain in such a cause. But being a white-collar man I know without proof that no laborer's toe could hurt more if stepped upon than mine. And who escapes getting stepped upon in this world?

Recently though I've discovered a palliative—at least for

the nights. Formerly the covers, even a sheet, would press down on my toe and cause such pain that I could not go to sleep. Then, perchance I did go to sleep, if I turned over or moved my foot and thereby dragged the covers the least bit, I would wake in such agony that I could not go back to sleep for the rest of the night. Now—I shall not tell you how it came to me—I discovered that if I put my foot in a waste-basket, the basket would hold the cover away from my foot. It worked so well the first night, in spite of the cold metal, that the next morning I went immediately after breakfast to the dime store where I had seen some plastic pails which seemed ideal.

I hurried into the dime store so that the man across the way in the health food store would not beckon to me. For how could I admit to such an enthusiastic man that wheat germ, liver, yogurt and blackstrap had little or no effect on the state of my toe?

Inside the store I wandered casually about before approaching, as though indifferently, the counter with the plastic ware. I looked at the medium-sized pails, measuring my foot mentally in the bottom. The salesgirl stood there silently, not chewing gum, but giving the appearance of chewing it, until I realized it was her tongue she was teething on to keep from laughing. She knew what I wanted the pail for. Yes.

"For forty-nine cents more," she said with feigned innocence, measuring my foot with quick, furtive glances, "we have this larger size."

"To hell with expense," I thought. "In a matter like this."

I looked straight at her as if it were merely a jockey strap I was buying and I was fourteen instead of forty. "Do you think a larger size would be better?"

"What color?" she asked as though that were the only remaining sensible question.

"It doesn't make any difference," I said; though secretly I wanted a rosy red one that looked both soft and warm. She reached toward the aquamarine.

I picked up the red. "May I have this one?"

"It's up to you. They're all the same price," she said and swished her tail over her head as she pranced to the cash register.

All afternoon I refrained from going to bed to try out the red pail. I must admit that I went an hour earlier than usual that night and slept beautifully until three A.M. It was not a sharp pain that awakened me then.

I was wide awake and thinking: What now if I should die in my sleep and should be found with my foot in a red plastic bucket?

LOCAL MAN FOUND DEAD:

MYSTERIOUS CIRCUMSTANCE

the *Evening Times* would decorously announce. But not so the Tabloid. With them a banner headline:

KARAKTER KONKS KICKING KAN

—which would be more appropriate, for it would seem, perhaps, odd to find a man dead or alive with his foot in a bucket. It would look, at best, like an accident: he had started to bed drunk and stepped in a bucket on the way. Not that I would mind the accusation if alcohol did anything except intensify the pain.

Well, you can't go back to sleep if you're afraid of being found dead in an undignified position. For some time now death and suicide have not been far from my mind. I have already made a will, burned all personal papers, got back from my wife letters written to her before our marriage and after our separation, reread and destroyed them, and filed all papers pertaining to my estate in a strongbox. All was, it seemed, in perfect order.

But suddenly, now, in the middle of this winter night I remembered a pack of pornographic playing cards given to me by a salesman on a train. I had meant to throw them away the minute I got off the train, but fear of detection prevented me. For four years they have been moved about, never once glanced at, from one locked place to another. But now, this night, they must be got rid of.

I finally find the right key and open the chest and look under the moth-eaten army sweater. A silver-bug slides along the edge and under the yellow newspaper.

There is no fireplace or stove to burn the things in. I take the cards into the bathroom and try flushing them four at a time. Thirteen flushes spaced between now and morning might not seem odd to the neighbors, unless of course they are awake and counting them all from the beginning.

But the cards float. It takes four flushes to get the first four down. No one, in the middle of the night, hearing fifty-two flushes would have to ask twice. I can hear him whisper to her: "He's getting rid of a pack of dirty cards."

Having no matches, I try tearing the cards to bits. The bits float. Then I discover that the bits, wadded up in aluminum foil, sink nicely. By dawn I am through with the whole pack in eighteen flushes, not counting the first four.

By noon I am across town at a different dime store. The new bucket does not match exactly in color or size, but it will do, and seems a miracle to me, this polyethylene bucket. Do you realize what progress we have made in this century? If, for instance, it had been the toe of my grandfather or even of my father, either of those gentlemen would have had to endure, night after night, cold, rattling buckets. Not me; my plastic pails are warm and silent.

Now, however, with a foot in each bucket, there is a problem in turning from stomach to back or even from side to side. The buckets are too large to roll over each other without disturbing all the covers and leaving a draft on my back. The only solution is to leave the buckets stationary and to change my feet from one to the other, which means I must either lie still all night, or wake almost wide awake if I want to turn over. Awake, or half-awake, my soul shrinks and I am glad that I had the wisdom to replace the gas stove (which could so easily and impulsively be turned on at such moments) with the electric range. And if I die the natural death I think of without fear, and am surprised dead, it will not look accidental—both feet in buckets. Maybe the coroner or insurance lawyer, prodding around, will take the clue and find on the dead toe some evidence that it had caused pain.

This morning, pretending to be charged with the burial of a distant cousin, I went early to a mortuary.

"The embalming process takes the blood from the brain also?" I asked.

"Oh yes, indeed," he said.

"Even from the fingertips?" I almost asked "extremities"; but then he would surely have known I meant toes.

"Every drop," he said.

I made him open the caskets as wide as they would open. He guessed I was interested in foot-room.

"Most people, unless they request otherwise, are buried without shoes," he said.

"Even so," I said, "these seem especially roomy."

"Extremely," he said.

Not that I feared that my toe, like a bad deed, would live after me. But I was overjoyed, nevertheless, when he showed me a casket that could be hermetically sealed. If not to me and my need, then to what purpose was it made? There is a glass plate which can be screwed tight and all the air can be pumped out and a vacuum created in the casket.

Surely in a vacuum, it can not go on—I can not go on—hurting.

The Tin Can

THEY WERE on the way back to the campus from the beach when the Blazer rear-ended them at a red light. At first it was his neck that seemed injured but the next morning he was in agony with a slipped disc in the lower back. Sally Gupton's little Mercedes sports car was totalled.

At first Sally Gupton seemed to have escaped without injury. "It takes more than a wreck," she said to him over the phone. "I've been in more danger in my own living room." She was almost sixty; her voice was gravelly as a road from years of drinking and shouting while surf fishing; her skin was leathery; and her hair uncontrollable even though it was cut as short as a man's. The students adored her, and at the moment, while she was offering to come and take him to a chiropractor, Jude did too. "I adore you, Gupton," he said into the phone.

"Damn it all to hell," she said, "don't get my blood pressure higher than it already is. Tom Kemp's threatening to put me in the hospital this afternoon." Her blood pressure was raging.

But why shouldn't he tell her he adored her: after all she had gotten him his job at the University and had shared her office with him. And fought all of his academic battles for him. She had nursed him through his divorce and two unhappy affairs. In five years they had not had a serious argument.

By noon the next day Sally Gupton was dead from heart fibrillation. She had written on the pad by her telephone, "I don't want to die. . . ." But they hadn't got her to the hospital before she was dead.

He was in such agony with his back that he had to leave the funeral service and for the next week or so he had told himself he would think about her when he could get out of pain. He was consoled by his last words to her.

The days had passed, the pain had subsided, he had begun returning to the campus, the classroom and the office he had shared with her; but he had not begun thinking about her. Even when he had to show her relatives which books were hers, which his, he did not really think about her as she had been alive.

But then a strange thing began happening to him. Sitting with his back to the window he would know, without turning around, that the Administration Building was gone. He did not need to turn and look out the window. He knew he could see straight across the site to the huge oaks on the front campus.

One day while talking with a student, the impression that

the Administration Building was gone, leveled to the ground, became so strong that under the pretext of adjusting the angle of the blinds, he had to stand and look out the window to be sure the building had not disappeared. For awhile the building stood quite solidly in his mind as he listened to the recitation, but when he began talking again the building disappeared again and again he stood to tinker with the blinds and to steal a glance at the building. "The sun isn't bothering me," the girl said.

"I'm catching a back glare in my glasses." He took off his glasses and wiped them as if the glare were still on them.

When the girl was gone he knew what he must do. He stood and, holding the building firmly in his gaze, thought for the first time, really, of old Gupton. Of a rainy midnight when she had knocked on his door wearing a yellow sou'wester, a huge yellow slicker that hid her completely. Seeing her through the glass panel, he thought it was a truck driver or someone needing a phone for emergency, but when he opened the door she came past him saying in her rough voice, "Dolly's thrown me out. All I want is a place to sleep until morning." Dolly was the woman she had been living with for twenty years. "Can I sleep on this thing?" She was already stretched out on a long couch and the room was already smelling of good bourbon and stale cigarette smoke. He made her get up while he peeled the wet raincoat off her and took the hat. When he got back with a blanket and started tucking her in she said, "I don't want mothering. I just need a place to sleep until morning." She was cursing Dolly and mumbling as she went off into a loud snoring sleep. The next morning she was gone and neither of them mentioned it again.

For awhile he thought he was through with his troubles but one day in the middle of a lecture he realized that the Adams Library with its great cupola had gone and that if he went to the window he would see only the tops of pine trees. He glanced a whole card ahead on his notes and walked to the classroom window still talking. By pressing his ear to the pane he should be able to see where the cupola had rounded into the sky. Much to his surprise it was still there. He returned to the rostrum still talking and by the time he flipped to the next card, the library had again disappeared. Toward the end of the lecture when he walked to the window again, there was a bit of uneasy whispering in the classroom, and a nervous giggle.

After class, after the last student had left, he went to the window and stared at the library roof. He imagined walking through the heavy glass doors and saying to the reference librarian in the Humanities room, "Tell me all you know about Sally Gupton."

He realized how private she had been behind that great

hearty exterior. Once he had asked her how she and Dolly had come to live together and she said, "Six of us had been playing tennis and we stopped in Harmon's for a Coke, and Dolly was with us. I'd never seen her before but when I ordered a Coke she said, 'You don't want a Coke. You want an RC Cola. You get twice as much for the same price.' That was when a dime was still hard to get. In graduate school. She told the waiter to bring me an RC. I knew that minute this was what I'd been waiting for all my life. Somebody who would tell me what to do."

For awhile everything was all right. Buildings stayed in their place, nothing disappeared. But then one night just after three he woke *up* thinking someone was banging on the door. In his waking sleep he thought it was Gupton. It seemed quite right and natural and even as he opened the door he expected her to be standing there. Instead he saw the shutter hitting the shingles. He tied it back but again under the covers, he could not sleep. When he shut his eyes he saw the light on the Bell Tower disappear and then the whole building, leaving the boxwood maze surrounding nothing.

He felt foolish, dressing and driving up to the campus and parking across from the Bell Tower in the middle of the night but it was better than lying alone sleepless. Gupton had told him about Gertrude Stein coming to the campus in the thirties and saying later that it was interesting that everyone took her to see the Bell Tower and all of them had said the same thing, "These boxwoods are little now. But someday they will be big." It was then he realized how much she loved Gertrude Stein. "If she hadn't come along it would of taken me thirty-five years to find out who I was and what I was about. No I never saw her but I'd have sold everything and gone to Paris just to meet her. But then I met Dolly." He was back in his bed and asleep in time to wake and turn off his alarm clock.

Later that winter in a meeting of the Faculty Council he had been humiliated. The South Quadrangle kept disappearing. Not just one building but the entire five. From the Faculty Club room he kept tilting back in his chair to see it again, and was paying no attention to proceedings in the room until he recognized the silence and saw the faces all turned toward him and heard the chancellor saying, "Maybe if we can have the attention of the Junior Faculty Member, we can bring it to a vote since there is no further discussion."

He sat with his face burning while he wrote his affirmative vote on the ballot. He folded the note, passed it on, and during the counting remembered Gupton saying to a shocked fundamentalist student, "No Miss Ryan, the woman in the story was not a harlot. Let's get one thing straight, Miss Ryan. In this class we call a spade a spade and a prostitute a whore. Don't try to protect yourself from literature or from experience with fancy words." Students had swarmed into the office to talk to her after class, but mainly to assure her they approved. So what if the girl wrote home, went to the dean as she threatened? It was obvious the students not only approved but that they loved her extravagantly. She was the maddest and the most honest person that had happened to them in their entire lives and the subject, obviously, of long speculations in the dorms. When he rushed out of the faculty meeting before anyone could speak to him, he felt like both laughing and crying when he saw the South Quadrangle, all five buildings intact. He walked on down to them and rubbed his hands along the rough brick and through the leathery ivy leaves.

Touching the building while thinking of her he felt was the secret, because for awhile no other building disappeared. But then he was shooting with some old classmates down near La Grange, Georgia, when he suddenly saw quite clearly the campus and the gymnasium. Next to the gymnasium was a bare red sloping hill, already eroding. What was missing? Something quite large. He tried several brick buildings but nothing fit the site. Then, as if on TV, the Tin Can flashed into view and in the next second was gone.

The Tin Can had been built as an armory and canteen, as a temporary structure in the First World War, but had proved so useful, always on a temporary basis, that it was still there in the sixties and later. When he first came here to the campus there was an indoor wooden track and in one corner a handball court and in the center Roman rings, high bars, gymnastic beams and horses, and in two different corners barbells and dumbbells. Half of the physical ed classes were still held in the metal shell which now claimed to be the largest, oldest temporary building on any college campus. During the thirties and forties the big name bands had played for dances there and many of the alumni were quite sentimental about it. Now it was missing.

He stayed on for the rest of the dove shoot, the eroding red clay site bothering him but not as much as if he had been on campus. As he drove back northward he could sometimes conjure up the Tin Can but usually it was the bare site that flashed before his mind. It was the ugliest building on campus, yet it had been a dormitory to a whole generation of football players; and the odor of sawdust and sweat was like no other odor on earth.

It was night when he reached the college town. He had driven four hours without stopping. There had been rain, and now for the last two hours patches of heavy fog. He was tired and hungry to the point of shaking. Yet he did not pull in at his own driveway, nor head for the restaurants on F Street. Instead he pulled into the gym parking lot and walked around that building toward the Tin Can. He stopped before knowing why: the Tin Can was no longer there in the stand of pines. He shut his eyes and lowered his head. Had he read they were taking it down during the holidays? For ten years there had been announcements and counter-announcements about its removal.

He opened his eyes and walked slowly toward the pines. There, sailing toward him in the heavy patch of fog, loomed the Tin Can. He ran toward the heavy barn doors, now secured with brass padlocks. He stumbled toward the lower corner away from the street and pressed his head against the cold sharp edge, and held with the palms of his hands to the cold wet sides. "Tin Can," he said, "don't leave." He was like a child trying not to cry. He slid along the side so that he was hidden from the street and the path and with his forehead pressed to the side of the building he cried and did not try to stop.

He cried for hurts and slights from all his life, but mainly he cried for Sally Gupton. He cried seeing her in her office, in her car, in her beach house reading at odd moments the prayer book she kept always with her. He cried because his wife had never loved him and he cried because he realized now that big old ugly Gupton always had. He cried because he saw how beautiful she was with her big awkward body and unruly hair. And he cried the way some students had cried in her class the day he announced the news of her death which he had not comprehended.

When he was done crying and feeling better than he had in a year, he slapped the building on the side, surprised by the rumbling echo, but he slapped it again nevertheless the way a husband might slap gently and playfully the rump of a wife beloved for half a century. With his palm still flat against the metal building he said, slowly and deliberately, "God bless you, Gupton."

As he turned and walked toward his car the sky was clear above the library cupola and the Bell Tower beacon was shining red against the stars. He felt as clean and healthy as if he had been swimming for an hour and as if the man crying against the building was someone he did not know and did not especially want to know. When he reached his car, he thought, ignobly it seemed to him, "Who will bless me?" In his peacefulness he put the self-pitying question behind him and he drove with confidence through the deserted streets of the campus blessing each building as he passed, knowing with certainty they would be there when he and all he knew were gone.

Color the Daydream Yellow

DURING THE two years when Roger Blair was married, living in Santa Monica, a graduate student at UCLA, he daydreamed (mainly after visits from Katherine's dykelike mother) about being single again and living in some great city: Paris once more, or Cairo, Athens, or Rome. In the daydream he had money to live, say, in Paris, on the Left Bank, and to drink on the Right. And the women in the daydreams were incredibly soft. In the large apartments he shared with them there was no rigid place for shoes, ties, raincoats, no exact time for breakfast, lunch, and so on, literally and so on.

Late that afternoon, the same as any afternoon, he glanced quickly up from his 3 x 5 note cards (Thomas Paine; Paris; In Pay of the French?) just as Katherine said: "We eat in two minutes. Okay?" Without even looking toward the red alarm clock on the terrible pink formica headboard (the bed cattycornered because there was no other way to reach the closet door and the clothes hanging in neat rows on hooks) he knew it was precisely two minutes till six. He lifted the card table–desk, the cards sliding, back into the corner in order to get out the door and into the other room, the "social" room which included Pullman kitchen, dining area, and "living" area.

Their calibrated life was resuming again. He tried to raise the venetian blind enough to watch the sunset over the Pacific as they ate. As usual the blind went up fast on one side and almost not at all on the other. The landlord who owned a dozen such student apartments would neither have the blinds retaped nor allow him to remove them. Today as they began (the hamburger was, as usual near the end of the month, smaller) the lower edge of the sun was already dissolving in the Pacific. Tomorrow at this same time it would be deeper under water and by midwinter completely gone at six o'clock, with no red streak of wave and cloud to remind one it had ever existed. "Color the experience red," he thought. They were still a little annoyed with each other and would not talk during this meal.

When she spoke she said, "It's 6:25." She meant: "Don't dawdle." She would insist on washing the dishes before leaving the house at 6:40 to be at the corner for the 6:45 bus. At 7:30 she would walk through the back door of the Wilshire Bank where she would sit until midnight playing the computers as if they were pipe organs. He had heard enough from her violent mother (who always imagined the worst possible things happening to her daughter) how dangerous it was for Katherine to be out catching buses after dark; and so now he walked with her to the corner and stood with her.

Tonight they were a minute or two early and waited without talking. It was a false sort of intimacy because she really was tired of the job and resented another year of graduate work ahead for him before she could quit. And all the time her mother, with the instant values of a waterfront whore, was putting ideas of divorce into her head, just as the old gal herself had got rid of Katherine's father. But she wanted Katherine pregnant first. The original Black Widow.

Katherine was nothing like her mother and seemed sometimes almost soft; such times as now when she gazed up the long street, her mouth not smiling, but pleased, with some inner secret. Often, in silence, their thoughts arrived at exactly the same point by wildly circuitous paths. He asked the familiar question, the utmost invasion of privacy which for some reason they allowed each other: "Where were you?"

"In Paris," she said.

"With me?" he asked. It would be nice if they could be back on, maybe not warm, but at least civil terms with each other.

"No," she said, a little annoyed, a little shy. "Before I met you."

"That Italian?" His face was flushing already with fury.

"What difference does it make?" She sounded edgy.

"This difference." Not he, himself, not any rational part of himself, but a fury took over his speech. "This difference: you mentioned it because you want a fight. Just as you get on the bus. So I'll be too angry to study. Well, I'll tell you one thing, you'd better come back on the bus and not let that fat idiot drive you. . . ."

Already the bus was pulling to the curb. "I hate you," she said.

"Not as much . . ." he started but then turned away and walked furiously toward the apartment. "Hell" he thinks and it is all he can think.

Sitting in the dark kitchen, a second cup of coffee before him on the table, he realized how foolish maybe he had been. Maybe at nine, during her coffee break, he would phone her. Apologize. Mention, if she sounded all right, how easy it will be to get a teaching job once he has the degree. Not that bluntly. Maybe just that his research is coming along great now. No, a simple apology: at least that, so they would not have to sleep another night without touching.

The ocean is black and only one star shines over it. He sees himself watching the black sky and sees himself two years ago, as lonesome then as now, regarding the sky over Paris. (Is it a daydream, the essence before an experience; or a memory, the essence after? And who can separate daydream, experience, memory and say which is which?) He watches the first sun rays find steeples, rooftops, the broad boulevards and sinuous river.

Below him on the lawn, an airline pilot with twenty hands, all rounded palms, is measuring a plump dark girl for a dress, stockings, brassiere, all of which he promises to bring on his next flight. The pilot is drunk, pretending to be sober; and she is sober, pretending to be drunk. And Roger Blair watching from his parapet, is alive, pretending to be a stone gargoyle, staring down with stone eyes at the embrace.

When he turns away, he finds exactly what during the night he had imagined: a dark-haired American girl with a guidebook, using the inlaid brass diagram to find in a systematic sweep the Trocadero, the Tower, the Military School, the Invalides, and the spire of St. Germaine. For awhile he helps her, but is defeated by her academic determination to see in two days all the French have built in twenty centuries. Besides which she must meet her mother at the American Express at nine. Maybe when she comes back from Italy, alone, in September, they can see some things together. She prints his name and Paris address in a neat leather notebook.

Such had been the day: the studious outsider looking in on the warm and warm-flushed couples (the Beaux Arts students, younger and wiser than he had ever been or would ever be, playing touching games with their lips and fingertips on the sunwarmed cobblestones sloping to the river); or wandering aimlessly or not courageous enough to admit an aim (from Montmartre to Montparnasse); making tentative approaches, his shyness frightening the young girls into a shyness which seems aloof.

"Ah now!" Roger Blair says, sitting down at last on a terrace near the Odéon. He stretches his legs until his desert boots are in the last remaining sun slanting down from the Luxembourg. Now at last, his feet are beginning to be warm; and into the pool of sunlight, two lizards, cleverly disguised as slippers, slide. He is absently studying the feet, the fine-boned tops and ankles, the tight black ski pants, when a voice says: "Can I have some of your sunshine?"

The accent is Swedish, husky, mournful, a winterful of nights, moons warmer than polar suns, a touch of bleak wind off a frozen lake.

He looks up quickly at her and quickly away. Thinks quickly of Garbo. No, that's ridiculous. Forgets her. Thinks of Grace Kelly. Forgets her. Sees the best skier he knows as she stoops to take the crest of a hill, then lets her fly out of sight. None of these. Seeks reality. Thinks of the boniest girl he ever saw swinging a racket in an awkward backhand. Sees all the tall girls he danced with out of pity at every high school dance. Shuts his eyes again and reconciles the images. Then dares to look again.

Is that high forehead with the heavy-lidded blue eyes and high cheekbones too strange, too oriental to be beautiful, framed by the incongruous silver blonde hair? Is the mouth too large, are the lips too pale and too full? The teeth too small? The neck, even in the black turtleneck sweater certainly is too long, as is the body with the small breasts. Later Roger Blair will ask for reassurance and will be told: "She's all right if the only thing you want is a handsome woman with flawless skin, perfect teeth, and elegant bones, along with a beautiful, sensual body."

What is confusing is this: she does not know she is exotic, delicious, elegant, all those things. She thinks of herself as shy, a little dull, boring, and has no pride in her looks. She is so convinced of her unattractiveness she convinces others of it. Or almost.

Roger Blair is confused only a moment and then moves his feet slightly to make room for her feet and says she can share his sunshine with him.

She is holding a leash and on the leash, asleep under an empty chair is a miniature schnauzer. It is not much of a dog but it is better than shyness and silence and so he asks if it is her dog.

"I keep him for my friend," she says the words cautiously in her heavy voice as if she is not at all sure the words mean anything at all. "And now they have runned off and lefted me."

Roger asks her in French if it has been a long time since they have abandoned her. She counts on the tips of a fan of fingers. "Un, deux, trois, quatre, cinq. Cinq. Cinq hours." She looks distressed but then smiles wistfully before looking distressed again. "I do not mind. It has been sun. But now the sun sits."

He orders a Dubonnet and when offered, she accepts a Coca-Cola. Wine, she has had so much wine all afternoon that now she is thirsty. Talk about Coca-Cola establishes him as an American and her as a Swede from Stockholm where Coca-Cola is also drunk.

"Isn't dot funny?" she asks with a smile too narrow and long. From a photograph one would suspect that the smile concealed bad teeth. But not at all. Evidently someone told her at eight that her mouth was too big; at twelve that she was too tall (hence the slightly stooped shoulders); her breasts too small (the loose sweater which flows about them when she moves); her feet too large—and there they were right. Yet it is her feet now that she has made no effort to hide, touching his with them lightly.

And during her second Coke ("oh my Got, but how I am thirsty!") Tilde's ridiculous plight is revealed in her great funereal voice: Lilibet, the girl she has come to Paris with from Sweden this very day, has left her here in this café while Lilibet and her French boyfriend, a medical student (named

Jean-Pierre of course) whom they met the summer before in Copenhagen, have gone off to find a room for the two girls. Lilibet's parents are very strict (the blue eyes roll at the thought of the puritanical parents) and Lilibet has promised them she will have a room. And now five hours have gone and the dog has not eaten and won't eat the roll she has tried to feed him. And Lilibet has all the money and their baggage is still at the station and she doesn't know how to get there and now she is afraid to leave. And the dog that belongs to Jean-Pierre! It is all so tragic as told.

"And," she announces after a long silence. "Do you know what Jean-Pierre calls the dog? Its name?"

He assures her he doesn't.

"Martini!" she is aghast. "Imagine, calling a dog 'Martini'." At the sound of his name the schnauzer thumps his stubby tail and rolls over in the sun. "Look at him," she says. "Joost look." The dog, warmed by the sun and his name, pretends to sleep again; he is grinning; he is dreaming; he is playing dead and does not know he is asleep. Roger Blair explains the dog to her and she is delighted.

She whispers: "Because he drinks martini and likes to be drunk." At the sound of his name the dog's ear twitches and as if to prove his lack of character, his sinful ways, he groans comfortably, opens one eye and shuts it again. The sober world is too much for him.

"My first day in Paris!" Tilde pouts.

Before they leave the café to buy meat for the dog, they write a note for Lilibet and Jean-Pierre; but when they come back at nine, after feeding the dog in the park and themselves in a bistro, there is a note from Lilibet saying Tilde should find a hotel room, just for the night. Tomorrow at noon they will all meet at the café.

To everything he has suggested, walking, shopping, eating, drinking, she has said "Yah!" easily and with no hesitation. So at ten, when she has yawned several great, wet-eyed yawns, he says: "Would you like to see my place?"

"Yah!" she says.

In silence they walk along to the Place St. Sulpice. There on the fifth floor, he points, is his apartment. On the sixth floor, his landlady lives in the maid's room when she is in Paris. Her light is on now and he does not want to see her tonight. Therefore it will be better if they do not talk on the stairs. "Yah," she whispers. "Yah!"

The next day as he slips out of the building he runs into his landlady talking to the concierge. Apparently she has been waiting for him all morning, though at the moment she seems absorbed in her mail. He gets almost to the street before she says: "Monsieur Roger." Will she ask him to move? Will she want more rent for an extra person? "Monsieur Roger, you do remember our agreement when you took the apartment?"

In his embarrassment he remembers nothing.

"No pets," she says, rather amused by her ambiguity.

His face grows warm.

"No dogs," she says. He is not sure.

"One can not risk fleas in summer," she says blandly and then there is a smile only in her voice. "A sympathetic young man like yourself can find better company than dogs I'm sure. So shall we agree again: no dogs?"

Thus begins the honeymoon. At the café Lilibet and Jean-Pierre are happy that the morose Swede will not be alone, and will that very day deliver her baggage and pick up Martini. When he arrives back at the apartment with red wine and cheese, bread and ham, Tilde is happy. "Yah," she says, sitting in the sun on the balcony. Even with her mouth full of bread and ham she can say it. "Yah. Is good."

Everything is good. "Yah," she says at night. "Yah. Yah." Until it almost becomes a playground taunt. "Yah yah yah." But the nights are the nights that a young man should experience if he is to be a complacent old man. "I have done my best and my best was good." But the mind seeks proof of its own sanity. Thus all honeymoons end; all plots thicken; every lover must have his rival (if Tilde is so marvelous as she seems, then other men must, by a lover's logic, see her as marvelous too); bliss without jealousy does not remain bliss. By its shadow we measure the height of a steeple. A steeple without a shadow may be no steeple at all. So now he needs to put in shade to make sunlight. He reaches for the black crayon:

And touches the fingers of Garcia Limon, Don Garcia Limon one would guess from the slight bow the Spaniard gives as he shakes hands. The Spaniard's hand is thin and strong. His clothes are genteel, shabby: suit jacket, tie, odd pants, pointed shoes, worn heels, polished. Son of a refugee. Medical student. Roommate, until the appearance of Lilibet, of Jean-Pierre. Now living in bleak poverty alone. Damn the sad eyes, the handsome brow and mustache, the dancer's body.

Torture time.

But if it is not Garcia Limon, the mind conjures another who sits at an unknown café, waiting for an unguarded moment to lure Tilde away. For now he knows "easy come, easy go" applies more to women than to money.

"Limon," Tilde says in the apartment. "He is nice. I like him. He is so poor. Lilibet and Jean-Pierre like him. He is nice." It is all she says.

But it is too much. He hears: "Limon is nice. You are not. He is poor. Therefore I like him, I feel sorry for him, I want to mother him, to feed him, to warm him with the warmth of my own body. Lilibet and Jean-Pierre like him better than they like you. Because he is nice."

He is silent.

"I am so tired." She stretches her arms into a wide bronze V above her body.

But why should she be so tired? It is only 10:00 P.M. and what has she done today? It is he who has made the bed, swept up, emptied the trash, marketed, cooked supper, stacked the dishes. What has she done besides bathe and wash her hair and dry it in the sunlight, lying naked on the plum colored velvet spread, her hair hanging down into the drop-rug of sunlight.

But while he was marketing, where had she gone? Today. Yesterday? Every day? For two weeks now. Isn't her explanation too strange? She can not stay in an apartment alone because once in Gottenburg as a student she returned from a weekend and found her landlord, an old man, a distant relative, dead, with the morning mail, the envelopes still unopened, about him like playing cards where he threw them in his fall toward the hearth. Who is to believe she leaves the house because the ghost of Cousin Augustus comes and rattles the skillets in every apartment where she is alone?

Now it is late July and the five of them have been swimming in the barge pool in the Seine. Garcia, Lilibet, Jean-Pierre, Tilde and himself. How soft, American, he seems amongst them with their thin, European, student bodies. The slightly immoral look of an athlete out of season, he sees himself, his own body. And as heavy in mind as body, trying to follow as they race across the verbal stepping stones from English to French and Spanish, resting on a German boulder before disappearing into a Scandinavian thicket, all laughing and understanding and waving kindly to him on his English shore. They come back for him as for a child and explain that he has missed nothing. It is unbearable. And what difference does it make if Tilde's shoulder is smooth and cool against his own if at the same time her warm toes are touching Limon's hairy thighs?

"But they weren't," she protests over hot chocolate in the middle of the night in the exact middle of the bed. "I don't know. I don't understand you. What if they were? Toes don't mean anything. *Toes!*" She exclaims something amusing (she claims untranslatable) to herself in Swedish. "Toes, my God!" She sits in the center of the bed hugging her knees. On her back the lamplight makes gold dust of the fine blonde hairs. "You are no fun anymore. At first you were fun."

Jean-Pierre when Roger finds him alone is no help. He says: "You are so serious. You're probably worse than those

Swedish men they come here to get away from." Jean-Pierre tries to explain: all winter it is dark, cold, unfriendly. Paris by contrast is a party. They dream of Paris, sunshine. Fun. They have not come down to get married. "Are you wanting to marry Tilde? Is that why you are so serious?" Roger Blair says he has not thought of it.

"Then how can you demand so much? Tilde thinks what you really want is a housewife. To make beds, sweep, wash dishes. Cook."

"Someone has to do it."

Jean-Pierre shrugs. Someday, Roger feels, he may hit a shrugging Frenchman.

"I know," Roger says. The truth is: at first, before the appearance of Limon, he did not mind that sort of housework. But now it adds to the silly picture he has of himself. He, out haggling for fresh eggs while Tilde sits somewhere listening to the motor-purr of Limon's Spanish-French.

The mind seeks before all things equilibrium. The bliss must not become too heavy or the scale will tumble, taking reason with it. Now Roger Blair adds, to the other side of the scale, his grievances: Garcia Limon and housekeeping. The two are really one, for if she kept house she would not have time to sit on a terrace with Limon.

"I sit in the sun," she states.

"It is strange no other sun is as warm as the sun where that Spaniard sits."

"Garcia likes the sun too." Tilde clips her toenails straight across and regards her biscuit-brown toes. "Yah, we are just alike, Garcia and I . . . me . . . we love the sun."

She loves fish for lunch and so he cooks fish for lunch and hates every bite she takes from her upside-down left-hand fork. He hates the way she raises her eyebrows and opens her eyes wide as she rakes the flakes of fish off the prongs with her small, even, bottom teeth. "Ah, it is so good!" she says now in her throaty voice. Only his cooking now receives such throaty compliments.

Then it happens, as he has imagined it would, and perhaps because he imagined it would. He comes by the café with a heavy net of groceries and she is not there waiting. Nor does she come home to supper. Nor is she there when he returns from a movie which he does not see, though he knows the shape of every blonde head in the audience.

At two o'clock, has he been asleep since midnight?, the light clicks on in the kitchen and he hears her voice: "Roger! Roger!" Tilde is afraid. A voice in a well. A whisper echoed in tile. Cousin Augustus may answer first. Certainly Roger Blair has no intention of answering. She enters still calling, as always, "Roger, Roger." The child-woman, infinitely appealing. Infinitely forgivable.

But not at 2:00 A.M. and where in hell will she say she's been? Oh, that she would only name the theatre where he has waited in ambush.

He pretends sleep, more silent and regular than sleep itself. Better than Martini had played dead. Apparently she sees his clothes, scattered over the living room, and stops calling. She pushes back the velvet draperies from the bedroom arch and crosses on bare feet. In the windowlight she glides and disappears behind the draperies that hide the bathroom door.

She emerges after a curiously long time, drying her hands in that peculiar nighttime way: pressed together as if for prayer but rubbed against each other, first in glee, and then for warmth.

"Get out," he says before she has a chance to sit down on the foot of the bed.

The argument begins, first in the dark, then in the light of the overhead fixture; they say absolutely nothing new in this argument, but the words are louder, more bitter and bitten, and finally she adds a new line: "I hate you."

He says it back to her: "And I hate you."

But though she does leave the apartment immediately, whoever parts for good on such fierce words?

Of course he tries to find her before she reaches the café. And of course she watches him running, then turns back and takes another street: toward Lilibet's and Jean-Pierre's; toward Limon's. He lets her go.

Now it is late August. The Paris shopkeepers have not yet returned from the South of France. The streets are hot and almost deserted. Flocks of American tourists, bright-colored and clear-voiced, descend suddenly on a street and light on terraces, tables and chairs. Off the main boulevards the little cafés continue with their habituals. Tilde now sits often where Roger Blair first saw her and often alone.

Sometimes Roger Blair sits at a table nearby or even at the same table if Lilibet and Jean-Pierre are present. Limon is in Spain and even if he comes back it is all right. Summer is at an end. Soon Limon and Jean-Pierre will be thinking only of their work; soon the Swedes will go back to Stockholm; soon Roger Blair himself will be leaving for New York or California. The world at the table is more tired than sad; more flat than round.

Lilibet to make conversation says to Roger: "The girl I saw you with yesterday, is she American?"

"The black-headed girl?" he asks, knowing it is Katherine she has seen.

"The most beautiful black hair, Tilde," Lilibet says. "Like we've always wanted. Long." She strokes imaginary tresses. "Black as ivory."

"Ebony!" Tilde says. "Yah?"

"Ebony, the black keys. As black as that."

"Yah!" Tilde says. "How beautiful!"

Are they teasing him?

"Oh," Tilde says, "how I have always wanted hair like that. What clothes you could wear! What hats! You can't wear hats with straw like this." She holds out her ponytail of sun-bleached hair. "Yah, beautiful." She turns directly to Roger. "Is she American?"

He nods, not trusting yet his voice to say she has been all summer in Rome.

"The one you used to mention sometime."

He shakes his head. "No. She didn't come over. She got married instead."

"I didn't like her," Tilde says. "She was so proper." They both are embarrassed a little by talk of the early summer. "Lilibet," Tilde says, "remember the time we rubbed carbon paper on our hair to make it black."

"And it came out marine blue. . . ."

"Purple!"

During their delight, Roger Blair leaves to arrange to meet Katherine the next morning. "In front of Sacre Coeur, then," he says over the telephone. "We can have breakfast in the nunnery behind the cathedral." He listens to her plans for the morning. Yes, he will take her to buy kitchen gadgets if that's really what she wants most to do. But tonight, dinner, she cannot change her evening. She must see an Italian friend who has been very nice and who wants to take her to a special restaurant.

He walks back to St. Sulpice satisfied. At least he will have someone to daydream about between pages of his book, sips of his brandy, puffs on his pipe. She is, he admits, even now he admits, pedantic, a real graduate student, not prim, but virginal, aggressively intellectual though soft-spoken. Nevertheless, her bottom lip is full and her eyes show mischief when they move too swiftly. It will not be easy.

He climbs the five flights to his apartment. Who would ever think of being homesick for an elevator? He sits with the windows open until the sky is darker than the mansard roofs, then turns on the tiny desk lamp which seems not bright enough to attract a moth.

Yet, within a few minutes, there is a fluttering at the door. Tilde, warmbodied and furry, enters, bumping the hallway, the doorway, the desk, before settling in the chair near the lamp. "Everything is so neat," she says. "Yah, like you like it."

It is the first time she has been back and she has dressed for the occasion: a soft white stole over a black cotton dress that looks like a petticoat. White cotton gloves that float near then far from her face and body.

How can he say to her: "I have another daydream going now?"

Back to America on the same boat, reading the same books, holding hands, nothing more, just holding hands with her till she gets used, first to his hands, then his cheeks, and gradually, maybe not even on the boat. Tilde does not belong in this dream. How to finish the first without having it overlap with the new one? Perhaps another argument?

"I am so hungry," she says.

So that is it. For a second the daydreams mingle and it is New York or California and Katherine is serving roast beef to him and Tilde. He looks out the window and the montage fades.

"I've been eating out," he says. Meaning: there is nothing in the house. "Since I planned to leave."

"Those good omelettes you used to make," she says wistfully.

"While you sat and did nothing," he wants to say; but that is the conversation that has become so hateful and slippery with repetition. "And the dishes I washed afterward," he wants to say, "while you slipped off to Limon." He is too angry to say anything.

"You always have something to eat in the house, here."

"Tea," he says. "That's all."

"Tea! Yah! Tea." She is delighted.

"Do you mind making it?" he asks. "While I change clothes?"

"You are going out." Her voice pleads and the melancholy note holds so that "out" goes on and on.

Until that moment he had not known he was. "Over to the Opera," he says.

Before he can take off his shirt, she calls to him from the kitchen. She can not remember where the tea is kept. He goes in. She is trying to heat water in a Pyrex bowl. It will be easier to make the tea for her than to mop up afterward; but she does not move from the tiny kitchen. "Go sit down, I'll bring it to you." She is entranced by something on the top shelf.

"Is that good to eat?" She points with white gloved finger to a can on a top shelf.

"It's beets," he says.

"They're delicious," she says. "I love them." She watches as he unbuttons his shirt. "I wish you did not go out tonight."

He reaches for the can of beets. "Do you want some?"

"If you open it for me. Those open-canners never work for me."

He opens the can and places a dish beside it and goes back to the bedroom to take off his shirt and to the bathroom to shave.

He comes out wiping the last of the lather from his chin and neck and chest. She is sitting at the desk. In the circle of light under the small lamp sits the open can of beets. As if she is daydreaming (does she see herself in a satin chaise longue, in white feathers and furs, lifting a bonbon from a box and while the maid massages her insteps, biting through the hard chocolate shell to the liquid cherry?) she reaches out and with delicate, gloved fingers dips into the can and lifts out, by its edge, a slice of pickled beet. She holds her other gloved hand under it as she brings it up, dripping, above her head and lowers it into her mouth. The red drops on the left glove spread out on the palm. She turns her hand admiring the polka dot effect. She swallows almost without chewing; then almost licks the stained glove finger. She looks up to see him watching and laughs, red fleshy bits of beets glistening as they slide across her teeth before being captured by the tip of her artful tongue. "Did you see me?" she asks. "I almost licked my glove."

Again, while he stands hypnotized, she fishes for another beet slice and dangles it above her mouth and cupped hand. "Yah, they are so good," she says and says something else that is munched up with the beet.

With her mouth full, studying her ruined gloves, she munches and laughs and tries to say something. "What a mess I am!" she finally says.

Such words have a final, definitive ring and it is on such casual phrases that lovers can finally part. He feels the daydream slipping. She glances at him as she reaches for another beet and sees herself dissolving, becoming thin, transparent, and nowhere.

"Don't you want one?" she offers him the can.

For a little while he wants to hold on to the dream, the memory, and so he takes a beet and eats it, wiping his mouth with the towel. Now she feels more real and moves toward him to test again her reality against his. The night is still dark when he wakes but she is gone.

So he lets Paris sink in the ocean wake, and lets himself walk now to the bow of the boat and think serious thoughts (What I Did on My Summer Vacation). In the deck chair behind him, he knows he has only to turn to see her, Katherine is stretched out, her neck bent, a book in hand, her black hair still brushed to a high sheen by the Swedish admiration, as pedantic and dull and essentially domestic as himself. No, he must not begin another daydream. Instead he must think serious thoughts and organize them well (What Do I Want Out Of Life?).

BEYOND THE kitchen window the ocean pitches black and white. There are no red waves and no red clouds to remind one the sun ever existed. Gradually, over the white ruffles of the waves he sees one star, and then another, until the sky and his brain itself seem to be dancing with them. The touch of the cold coffee cup to his lip startles him and he is frightened. For a little while he has been outside himself, for a little while he has cleared his head of all thought, his heart of all anger; and he feels both weak and drunk. Where was he? Where is he? What was he thinking? Paris? Is he in Paris imagining a girl named Katherine, or in California imagining a girl named Tilde?

And Katherine, was she part of a daydream once or is she a memory too? Was it really two weeks ago she got on the bus? And the supper tonight, was it merely a sweet memory of all their suppers? Or was it tonight she got on the bus and is he merely daydreaming that she has left him?

He tells himself not to panic. In the blue glow from the pilot light on the stove he can see the dish drainer. The dishes: two plates, two salad bowls, two glasses, two knives, forks, spoons, two saucers, one cup, all neatly slanted, still spotted with water. Through the doorway to the bedroom he can read the luminous dial of the travelling clock. Thank God, he still has time to get to the drugstore and call her at her coffee break. He will meet her at the bank and buy her a beer. Yes, and over the phone he will tell her he loves her so she will be through with her crying when he tells her again in the bar.

For a moment longer he sits at the table and fills in the outlines of familiar objects with familiar colors. "Color the dish drainer white. Color experience red and color the dream blue; color the daydream yellow and memory green, and shade one into the other like lights on water. And if one fades into the other or even if the colors run together, it will last only a little while. For like the ocean, soon it will be all dark. Then color my soul red and color me quick!"

Look for these Algonquin
Front Porch Paperbacks at your local bookstore:

The Cheer Leader by Jill McCorkle
ISBN 1-56512-001-9 $8.95

July 7th by Jill McCorkle
ISBN 1-56512-002-7 $8.95

The Queen of October by Shelley Fraser Mickle
ISBN 1-56512-003-5 $8.95

Music of the Swamp by Lewis Nordan
ISBN 1-56512-016-7 $7.95

Daughters of Memory by Janis Arnold
ISBN 1-56512-031-0 $9.95

Passing Through by Leon Driskell
ISBN 1-56512-056-6 $8.95